A Candlelight Ecstasy Romance®

"YOU AGREED TO THE BET. NOW YOU'LL HAVE TO LIVE WITH IT."

Keely swallowed hard. "But I don't want to live here . . . as your . . . wife!"

A grin slowly spread across Tyler's face. "What's the matter, Keely. Have you forgotten how to . . . cook?"

"Cook? That wasn't what I was thinking of."

"I know what you were thinking, and that's entirely up to you whether you want me to be your 'husband' for a week or not. I'm game. We never had any trouble in that area."

Keely sprang up in self-defense. "If you think I came here to sleep with you for a week, then turn around and go back home and get a divorce, you're crazy. How dare you—you inconsiderate . . ."

"All right. Forget it. The bet doesn't include bedroom privileges. All I ask is your culinary art."

"Well, I never . . ."

"You're right—not with me, unless you beg!" His grin widened. . . .

A CANDLELIGHT ECSTASY ROMANCE ®

ALL
OR
NOTHING

Lori Copeland

A CANDLELIGHT ECSTASY ROMANCE ®

Published by
Dell Publishing Co., Inc.
1 Dag Hammarskjold Plaza
New York, New York 10017

Dell ® TM 681510, Dell Publishing Co., Inc.

Candlelight Ecstasy Romance®, 1,203,540, is a registered
trademark of Dell Publishing Co., Inc.,
New York, New York.

ISBN: 0–440–10120–4

Printed in the United States of America
First printing—February 1984

To Norma Brader, who's been more than a friend.
And special thanks to W. D. Blackmon
for his expertise in English.

To Our Readers:

We have been delighted with your enthusiastic response to Candlelight Ecstasy Romances®, and we thank you for the interest you have shown in this exciting series.

In the upcoming months we will continue to present the distinctive sensuous love stories you have come to expect only from Ecstasy. We look forward to bringing you many more books from your favorite authors and also the very finest work from new authors of contemporary romantic fiction.

As always, we are striving to present the unique, absorbing love stories that you enjoy most—books that are more than ordinary romance.

Your suggestions and comments are always welcome. Please write to us at the address below.

Sincerely,

The Editors
Candlelight Romances
1 Dag Hammarskjold Plaza
New York, New York 10017

CHAPTER ONE

"If you want a divorce, you'll have to come and get it!"
The loud click on the other end of the phone left no doubt
that Tyler Jerico was finished with the conversation.

"That inconsiderate . . . horse's patoot!" Keely slammed
the receiver down in agitation, her blue eyes blazing with
fire.

The tall, gray-haired man standing at the file cabinet
chuckled quietly under his breath as he extracted a long
yellow file from the cabinet and turned around to face his
flustered daughter cautiously. "I gather you love birds"—
he paused and chuckled again, then continued in a teasing
Irish brogue—"didn't take to each other again today."

Keely slammed a folder down on the top of her desk in
exasperation. The slight flush on her face, which featured
her large eyes and was framed in long sable brown hair
that fell just below her waist, only accentuated her loveliness. For, when one looked at Keely Jerico, that was the
first word that popped into one's mind—lovely. Of course,
one could also add stubborn and hot-tempered as well as
loving and generous to that list, but one would have to
really get to know Keely before those attributes emerged.

"That undoubtedly is the most stubborn man I have

ever met in my life!" she fumed, slamming her desk drawer shut for emphasis.

Devin Majors's weather-lined face broke into a broad grin as he walked over to the coffeepot and poured his ninth cup of the day, ignoring the frown that gathered on his daughter's face. "With the possible exception of one person, I think you may be right," he said, looking at her pointedly. He stirred three teaspoons of sugar into the hot mixture and with his blue eyes twinkling, observed good-naturedly, "Ty wasn't too enthused about it, I gather?"

"Oh, he's enthused about it all right." Keely paused and put on her most somber and authoritative face. "If you want a divorce, you'll have to come and get it!" The tone of her voice sounded amazingly like her tall, handsome husband's now as she got up to pace restlessly around the small floor in the office of her father's construction firm, the heels of her shoes tapping out a rhythmic pattern on the wood floor. "That pig-headed, stubborn, ill-mannered . . ."

"Now, wait a minute, honey. There's no sense in getting yourself all bent out of shape over him again. Just calm down and tell me what he said." Devin Majors seated his daughter on a small couch that stood against the wall in the small room. He lowered his large frame down beside her and reached for her hand, patting it lovingly. "Now, calmly, what did Tyler have to say about the divorce?"

Keely buried her face in her hands tiredly, the emotions of the last few minutes draining her completely. The last six months had been a constant drain on her nerves, loving her alienated husband one minute, and hating him the next. That's why, after endless hours of soul-searching, she had come to the conclusion that she could no longer go on in this state of limbo. It was obvious they were not going to be able to work out their marital problems, as much as she desperately wanted them to. She had too much pride to beg Tyler to take her back. No, she had vowed silently, *he* had been the one to storm out on their

10

marriage, and *he* would be the one to return. But as the months went by, he hadn't returned, and Keely's hopes began slowly to fade. The few times they had talked by phone to each other had been disastrous, each one blowing up in anger with the other.

"I just don't know what to do, Dad," Keely sighed as she leaned her head against the dark plaid of his broad shoulder. "Maybe you are right. Tyler and I are too much alike . . ." her voice trailed off helplessly as unwanted tears dripped silently from her anguished eyes.

"Now, now, darlin'. Don't start those tears again," Devin pleaded helplessly as he began to gently stroke the lustrous brown curls that hung riotously down the back of his only child, murmuring softly now as her tears increased. "Ah, Keely girl, you remind me more of your mother every day. All hot and fiery one minute, then soft and warm the next." He sighed painfully as old memories tore at his heart. "When your mama died, a big part of me died with her." He patted Keely consolingly on the arm. "I know what you're going through, girl, and if I could ease the pain for you, I would, but this is something that you and Tyler are going to have to work out between yourselves."

His voice took on a sterner tone as he pulled her around to face him, taking a large white handkerchief out of his back pocket and handing it to her. "And if you ask me, neither one of you has tried hard enough to solve whatever went wrong with your marriage. You're both too darn stubborn!"

Keely sniffed irritably and grabbed the handkerchief from his hand to wipe hurriedly at her eyes, trying to keep up with the rapid flow of tears. "You know perfectly well what went wrong. It's his *stupid* jealousy that tore this marriage apart! If you ask me, I think he was simply looking for an excuse to end the marriage the night he found me having dinner with Craig."

"Now, honey, you have to admit, it did look suspicious.

11

You and Craig in a quiet, romantic restaurant, having dinner after you deliberately told Tyler you were working late," he reminded her, his voice growing angry.

"But I *was* working late, Dad. Oh, I know I should have told Tyler the truth—that Craig had insisted on a working dinner meeting before he signed the contract, but that's *exactly* why I didn't tell Tyler—because I knew he would misconstrue the meaning of the meeting and his jealousy would override common sense, which is exactly what happened!" Keely pointed an accusing finger at her father. "And if *you* hadn't constantly tormented Tyler about Craig being in love with me before Tyler came into my life, he wouldn't have been so insanely jealous!"

Devin hung his head in shame, the truth of her words hitting home. He had teased Tyler unmercifully about Craig's infatuation for Keely, but he had never fully realized the enormity of Tyler's possessiveness until it was too late. It had become almost a sickness with Tyler, the last few months of their marriage becoming a virtual battleground between Tyler and his daughter. Devin shook his head slowly in sad remembrance of the tall, quiet man he had hired one rainy day a little over two years ago.

Tyler had shown up at the construction site, looking for work, on a gray morning in December. Devin had hired him instantly, taking a deep liking to him. He was a hard worker, a man who obviously knew the construction business inside and out. Tyler immediately set his cap for the owner's lovely daughter, and she, in turn, fell head over heels in love with him. They made a stunning couple—he with his coal black hair and eyes the color of cool steel. His six-foot-plus frame towered handsomely over her petite and dainty loveliness. Love radiated from their faces with such clarity that Devin had no qualms about giving his daughter's hand in marriage to a man he barely knew.

Tyler obviously worshipped the ground Keely walked on. Tyler had no family. He had been raised in a succession of foster homes and had no one whom he was close to, so a small wedding was arranged one beautiful spring day in April just four months to the day from when they had met. The sun shone bright on the happy couple the day of the wedding, and everything was right in their world.

Devin shifted on the couch, his eyes resting on Keely's bent head. His dreams of Tyler and Keely taking over the business and the grandchildren to come had filled him with joy. Now he wasn't sure when he first saw signs of his dreams begin to fade. Before his eyes, Tyler and Keely's marriage slowly, but surely, began to fall apart at the seams.

Craig Easton had dreams that revolved around Keely before Tyler came along. Devin seriously doubted that Keely ever returned those feelings, although she had dated him steadily before her marriage. Craig was surprised and shocked when Keely announced her intention to marry Tyler. He could never quite adjust to the loss of the woman he had wanted. Even after the marriage, Craig made no secret about the way he still felt about Keely. Keely avoided him as much as possible, but Craig was a well-respected businessman, and the Majors Construction Company relied on doing a great deal of business with him. Tyler made no effort to conceal his dislike of Craig Easton, and many an argument erupted in the small construction office after hours between Tyler and Keely about Craig. As the months sped by, Devin watched the quarrels grow more heated, with Keely's stubbornness clashing with Tyler's obstinacy. After that debacle in the restaurant, Tyler had returned to Colorado, where he had originally come from, and Keely tried valiantly to pick up the pieces of her shattered heart. Devin had watched his daughter and son-in-law with a heavy heart as the months crawled by, both of them letting their stubbornness widen the gap between them. Keely lost weight, and her smile lost its spontaneity. Devin remembered the day she confessed to him in a crying fit that she couldn't live with Tyler and couldn't live without him.

Devin shook his head worriedly, recalling his trying to talk some sense into her. When that failed, he had called Tyler, trying the same approach with him, but met with the same results. Sheer bullheadedness on both their parts! He had finally washed his hands of the whole matter, never mentioning the ill-fated marriage again until Keely had told him this morning that she had finally seen a lawyer and had divorce papers drawn up. He had listened with a sense of despair as Keely called Tyler to inform him that she was sending the papers in the mail for him to sign. True to form, Tyler had refused to sign them.

"Well?" Devin asked. "Are you going to him? I could go with you, you know."

Keely pushed herself up from the small couch and resumed her pacing, her face a mask of indecision. "I don't know, Dad. I don't know if I can go out there and engage in another battle with him. The marriage is over. I don't want to see him again."

Keely stopped her pacing and stood staring out the small window at the bright fall sunshine. That wasn't quite true. She did want to see him again. She couldn't help it. More than anything, she wanted to see that tall, completely masculine husband of hers just once more. She longed to gaze one final time into those silver eyes that could become so warm and alive with desire. There had certainly never been anything lacking between them in their sex life. On the contrary, they could never seem to get enough of each other. A tiny smile feathered the corner of Keely's mouth as she thought of all the lazy Sunday afternoons they had spent in bed, each one teasing the other with their mouths and hands to the point of near madness until their eager bodies would meet in ecstasy. A tiny shiver rippled over Keely as the tears welled up once again in her eyes. So much of their marriage had been perfect. Why couldn't it have all been lazy, romantic Sun-

14

day afternoons? She turned back from the window, wiping the tears away with the back of her hand.

"No, Dad, I don't want you to go with me. There's too much to be done here. I'm a big girl now. I should be able to face my own husband." Keely managed a weak smile. "I'll fly down there and get Tyler's signature on the papers and fly back. I'll only be gone overnight." Somehow she felt better just making the decision. She would book a flight out on the next plane, have Tyler sign the documents, then catch a return flight the following morning. Once the papers were signed, it would be easier.

"Are you sure, darlin'?" Devin stood to enfold her in a big bear hug of assurance. "It wouldn't be any trouble for me to go with you, you know."

Keely hugged her father back tightly. "I'm sure, you big softie. You stay here and build buildings. I'll go off to war," she teased lightly.

"Yeah, well, you're probably right about that!" Devin said, grinning devilishly. "The poor unsuspecting people of Colorado better start running for cover when your plane hits the landing strip, 'cause there's sure to be fireworks when the Jericos unite again!"

He loosened his arms around her, his face turning somber. "All I want is your happiness, honey. Nothing more. Just be *sure* this is what you want."

"Thank you, Dad." She gave his weathered neck an extra hug before stepping back from him. "It's what I want." Keely mentally crossed her fingers for telling her father the slight fib. It wasn't what she really wanted, but what choice had that pigheaded husband of hers left her?

As Keely fastened the seatbelt for the landing, she mentally reviewed the scant information Tyler had given her about where he was now living. As the large plane touched down on the runway, she recalled that the address he had given her was a condominium just outside of Colorado Springs. She knew that her husband was now a partner

15

with a man by the name of Chris Morgan in their own construction firm.

The jet taxied smoothly alongside the terminal and eased to a halt. Keely emerged with the other passengers, her stomach reminding her she hadn't eaten since the day before. The thought of seeing Tyler again after six months made her knees weak and her stomach queasy.

Maybe I should get a sandwich before I call him, she thought uneasily as she reached for the one light suitcase she had brought with her. Or, better yet, maybe she should just check into a hotel and put the call off for a little while longer. Coward! A little voice tormented. *No! I'm not a coward,* Keely reasoned angrily. It was just that she never ate before a flight, and she was extremely tired from the lack of sleep the night before. She had lain awake most of the night dreading the prospect of seeing her husband again, yet just a little excited.

She sat down a minute on one of the leather chairs that lined the airport terminal and tried to gather her wits. Her eyes spotted the long line of telephones; they seemed to challenge her. She sat staring at them for a full five minutes, chewing her lower lip in indecision. Finally, with a deep sigh of resignation, she dug in her purse for some loose change and a small slip of white paper with his business phone number hastily scribbled on it. She dropped two coins into the slot, and took a deep breath.

"I'll call, and while the secretary is getting him on the phone, I'll try to think of what to say to him," she mumbled sensibly.

The phone rang a couple of times before she heard a brisk voice bark, "Jerico here."

Her blood froze momentarily as she recognized the deep timbre of Tyler's voice. Her mouth felt like cotton, and her knees turned to liquid as she closed her eyes and sagged weakly against the small telephone booth. Suddenly all her anger was gone. The sound of his deep voice, that husky voice she had heard so many times whisper softly into her ear in moments of passion, caused a swift stab of pain to course through her. She swallowed and took another deep breath. "Uh . . . why are you answering the phone?"

There was a brief moment of silence before Tyler answered cautiously, "My secretary, Sheila, isn't here right now."

"Oh," came her weak reply.

There was a moment of silence from the other end before he stated dryly, "Didn't take you long, did it?"

"Uh . . . long . . ." Keely was finding it hard to talk. She wiped the palms of her sweaty hands on the sides of her skirt.

"What's the matter? Is Craig that anxious to make an honest woman out of you?" The sarcasm in Tyler's voice was evident.

Keely suddenly began to snap out of her stupor as the sound of his arrogant voice reached her.

"For heaven's sake, do we have to start this over the phone? Good grief, Tyler, I haven't even said who's calling!"

A dry, mirthless laugh followed. "Do you honestly think I wouldn't know my own wife's voice?"

"May I remind you, Tyler, before this goes any further," she said in a warning tone, "I didn't *have* to come. I *could* have had my lawyer bring these papers down for you to sign!"

"The hell you didn't," Tyler said calmly. "I told you in plain English, you either brought those papers down for me to sign or you could take them and—"

"You don't need to tell me your exact words, Tyler," Keely interrupted. "I remember what you said. It seems to me you could use a little nicer language when talking to a lady!" she added heatedly.

"I do," Tyler said placidly, "when I'm talking to a *lady.*"

17

Keely was growing very tired of his sarcasm. "Look, I'm at the airport."

"So?" came the bored reply.

"What?" Keely didn't think she had heard him right.

"I said, so? What do you want me to do about it?"

"W-well . . ." Keely stammered, "do you want to come out to the airport and sign the papers, or should I check into a motel, where you can come by later?"

"Suit yourself," he replied crisply. "It's your party."

She was beginning to do a slow burn. He was as asinine as ever! "I don't *suppose* you'd recommend a nice hotel."

"You supposed right. Why don't you call Craig and ask him?"

Keely ignored his taunt. "I'll call a cab, then check into a motel. Do you want me to call you later?"

"I'm too damn busy to fool with you today, Kelly," he snapped.

"Well, *excuse* me! It seems I'll have to send my lawyer after all," she replied hotly.

Keely started to hang up as she heard Tyler bark gruffly, "Keely!"

"Yes?" He'd better not say he had changed his mind and was going to come out to pick her up. She wouldn't go with him now if he offered to carry her piggyback to his office!

"Take a cab out to my apartment, and I'll meet you there when I'm through for the day. There's an extra key under the slot in my mailbox."

"What time will that be? I'd like to return to my motel early and rest. It's been a long day," Keely told him coldly.

"It will be when I damn well want it to be!"

The sharp click of the phone stuck in Keely's ear. "That insufferable bore is beginning to make a habit out of hanging up on me!" Keely mumbled, slamming the phone back on its cradle.

Still seething, Keely swiped up her suitcase and hand-

18

bag and made her way out the front door of the terminal. Several minutes later she was seated comfortably in a cab, speeding along under the brilliant blue of the Colorado sky.

Her anger dissipated swiftly as she watched the breathtaking landscape sweep majestically by her. The brilliantly vivid colors of the changing aspens held her spellbound, the trees proudly displaying their fluttering leaves. The awe-inspiring Pikes Peak stood just east of the city, its towering peak capped with snow. Keely's eyes focused on the beautiful leaves fluttering to the ground in the gentle breeze. How could some things be so beautiful as they were dying, Keely mused as the cab sped along the quiet residential street taking her to Tyler's home. Her marriage was dying, and it certainly was not beautiful.

Why couldn't her pending divorce be a happier prospect for her? She should be thrilled to be getting rid of that stubborn man! She didn't know what had ever made her think she could love someone whom she was constantly at odds with. Well, to be truthful, they hadn't *always* been at odds, she admitted silently. They had had their good times, and not just in the bedroom. They had laughed together, played together. But the bad times began to outnumber the good ones. Those times when Tyler's jealousy had exploded, causing fight after fight. She fully realized now she could not live with a man who didn't trust her. He had made a mockery of her vows to him.

What puzzled Keely the most was the fact that she could never understand why Tyler felt so insecure about her love. From the day they first met, there had been no other man for her. And the matter of Craig Easton was so absurd that she saw red every time an argument erupted over him! Keely had liked him well enough, but she had never entertained the idea of anything serious between them. She was aware that he had hoped for more, but she had reminded him gently on several occasions that she didn't really feel there would ever be anything more than

19

friendship for them in the future. He had smiled and said, "I can always hope, can't I?" But Tyler wanted to read more into that relationship than had ever existed.

Keely sighed as she closed her eyes momentarily. Her dad had not made it any easier on her either. He had constantly teased Tyler about Craig's infatuation for her. She didn't think her father ever really realized how upset Tyler would become after one of those teasing sessions in the small construction office. They would drive home to their apartment in uneasy silence, and before the evening was over, Tyler would have found some reason to pick a fight with her. Keely sensed a deep sense of insecurity in him, yet she had never been able to talk with him about it. He would always dismiss the idea, turning a cold shoulder to her, never opening up to her as she so fervently wished he would.

The evening Tyler walked into the restaurant and found her having dinner with Craig was the breaking point in their year-old marriage. After Tyler stormed out, Keely had a concise conversation with Craig and immediately called a cab and followed Tyler home to try to explain. She realized how foolish it was on her part not to let Tyler know she would be having a business dinner with Craig. With tears in her eyes she had pleaded with him to listen to reason, but he refused, and in the early morning hours had raged out of the apartment, leaving her alone, confused, and frightened.

Well, that was all behind her now. After today she would have his signature on those divorce papers, and Tyler would be out of her life forever. Luckily there were no children to tie them together in the future. Not that they hadn't wanted a child. On the contrary, Tyler had confessed that he loved children and would like nothing better than to have his own. He had spent so many unhappy years being shifted back and forth between foster homes after his parents died that he longed for the security of a home and family of his own. Keely could feel the faint

20

stirring of tears beginning to surface as she remembered the one and only Christmas they had spent together and how like a child he had been. They had put up a traditional tree and decorated it on Christmas Eve, its tiny multicolored lights blinking brightly in their small apartment. Tyler had tried to hide his eagerness to open his gift from her, but had failed miserably. She had deliberately made him wait until Christmas morning to open the beautiful gun that she had bought him, one he had admired for many months when they went into the local gunsmith's. He had begged pitifully to open it on Christmas Eve, but his pleas fell on deaf ears.

"You have got to be the cruelest woman I have ever encountered," he whispered petulantly as he came up to slip his arms seductively around her slender waist. She had been fixing them a cup of eggnog in the kitchen around midnight. His hands began to stroke suggestively along her stomach, his lips trailing soft kisses up and down her neck.

"You only have to wait a few more hours, Tyler," she said consolingly, her breath catching slightly as his hand came up to capture one of her breasts. Gently he began to stroke the budding softness with tantalizing sureness, his breath warm and moist on her throat.

"I'll give you *one* of my presents early," he murmured in a low timbre, rubbing suggestively against her bottom. His hand was now exploring down the waistband of her slacks. "If you'll just let me open that *one* long package all wrapped in red."

Keely grinned impishly, cold shivers coursing through her body as his fingers caressed her intimately, his hand teasing lightly on the inside of her thigh. "You can open the small box wrapped in blue," she offered, moving her neck closer to his playful mouth.

Tyler sighed in mock exaggeration. "But I don't want to open the *blue* box." His lips and hands were working magic on her body now as she leaned back to press against

21

his taut thighs. The growing sign of his masculinity was evident as she turned in his arms, her hands going up lovingly around his neck.

"I want to open the *red* box," he persisted as his lips left hers to nibble at her earlobe.

"Uh-uh." Keely held firm. Her hands explored the hollows of his back now. "I'm sorry, I can't let you do that. There's a sticker on it that says Do Not Open Until Christmas. It would be almost like tearing one of those tags off a bed pillow. I would probably be subject to penalty under law if I let you open that *red* package tonight. You understand, don't you, Ty . . ." Her hands were busy unbuttoning the top two buttons of his dark blue sport shirt.

He groaned softly as she slipped her hand into his shirt to run her fingers smoothly through the dark hair that grew in a thick patch across his broad chest. "Then I won't give you one of yours early," he threatened as his mouth caught hers in blistering kisses. Keely's knees grew weak as they stood in the small kitchen, Tyler devouring her mouth with his.

"Ah, come on, Tyler," she whispered softly between one of his searing kisses, the tip of her tongue tracing the outline of his lips moistly, "you know I *can't* let you open your present, but are you *sure* you don't want to give me *one* of mine?" She rubbed suggestively up against his obvious desire for her.

Tyler's cool gray eyes had turned dark and cloudy as her slender fingers reached down to begin very slowly to unzip his tailored dark blue trousers, her tongue moving to his ear, her lips nibbling gently at the lobe.

"You're playing dirty, Keely," he whispered hoarsely, his hands slowly beginning to undress her. The quiet sound of his zipper coming down, and the soft swish of her dress hitting the floor could be heard over the soft Christmas carols playing on the stereo.

"Mmm, I know," she said, tantalizing him.

Their kisses turned into an inferno as Tyler lifted her

into his arms and carried her over to the sofa in front of the blazing fire. He hurriedly stripped out of the remainder of his clothes, then joined her on the couch. His breathing became labored as the firm, lean contours of his body blended with the soft loveliness of her naked curves. Their mouths joined hotly once again as his hands moved urgently over her body, stroking, urging, and exploring every inch of her.

"I love you, my beautiful wife. I love you," he moaned against her mouth. "You're my whole world, Keely, and I love you."

"I love you too, Tyler," Keely whispered, tears of happiness forming in her blue eyes. "Merry Christmas, darling."

"This is your stop, lady." The voice of the cab driver broke through Keely's tortured thoughts as she became aware of her surroundings once more. The cab was stopped in front of a two-story red brick apartment building.

"Oh . . . yes, I'm sorry." Keely rummaged in her purse for some money. Handing the driver a twenty-dollar bill, she reached blindly for the handle on the door, a fine mist of tears blurring her vision.

"Hey, lady! You've got change comin'."

Keely looked back at the face of the tired cab driver. "Just keep it," she called over her shoulder as she walked hurriedly up the sidewalk to the tall building. She let herself into the entryway and walked over to the row of mailboxes. Finding the one that read Tyler J. Jerico, she slid her fingers beneath the small metal box, coming up with a silver door key. A few minutes later she stood in front of a large wooden door marked Apartment Two. Sliding the key into the lock, she swung the door open.

Keely's mouth dropped open as she came face-to-face with the largest great Dane she had ever encountered. He was sitting directly in front of the door, his massive body

23

tense and alert. The low, telltale growl emanating from his throat warned Keely that he was in no mood for unexpected company.

Keely swallowed hard and grinned at the hairy beast. "Hi, doggie." The dog's large brown eyes glared at her sternly.

"Good doggie," Keely said, taking a hesitant step into the room, her eyes never leaving the menacing creature. The growl grew a little louder as the door swung shut, leaving Keely and the dog in the room, both sets of eyes locked in visual combat. Why hadn't Tyler warned her he had a—the word *dog* seemed inappropriate for the colossus sitting in front of her, the strong massive body not budging an inch from his undisputed territory.

Keely edged carefully over to the chocolate brown corduroy sofa sitting in the middle of the room, dropping her suitcase on the floor. The dog suddenly sprang to his feet, his growl turning serious now. Cold sweat popped out on Keely's forehead as the dog apparently decided to let it be known who was calling the shots from now on. Not that Keely would have disagreed with him in any way. On the contrary, he was the boss, and she knew it.

The dog edged closer to her as she held her breath. Her eyes widened with fright as he plopped down not two feet away, his fierce brown eyes warning her he would not stand for any "funny stuff" on her part.

Smiling sickly, Keely assured him in a weak voice, "It's all right, doggie. We'll just wait until your master gets home. I'm in no hurry. I'll just sit here." The dog's eyes assured her that she was absolutely correct. She would sit there!

"Yes, sir," Keely said matter-of-factly, beginning nervously to smooth the pleats of her oatmeal-colored suit skirt. "I'll just sit here and wait until your master comes home. I'm sure he'll be here any minute now." She glanced hurriedly at the clock. It was after six. It surely wouldn't be long now—she hoped!

CHAPTER TWO

Maybe it's a small breed of horse, Keely mused forty-five minutes later as she sat in the same position on the couch. Her body was growing numb from sitting so long. Every time she had moved the slightest bit, the dog had emitted a low growl, getting to his feet to stare hostilely at her. She glanced for the hundredth time at the small clock sitting on the marble mantelpiece. Seven o'clock and Tyler still hadn't shown up! *He's probably purposely doing this to let me know how low his opinion of me is,* Keely fumed. *He's undoubtedly having a good laugh right about now thinking how upset he has me. Well, Mr. Jerico, you're not bothering me one bit! It's this damn dog that's bothering me!*

"Hey, dog." The dog raised his brown eyes to meet her defiant blue ones. "What's your name?" she asked curtly.

The dog laid his head back down on his paws, trying to ignore the tense object sitting before him.

"Let's see. Is it Killer? Masher? Oh, I know—Mangler?"

The dog's large eyes closed wearily. Keely started to ease herself into a different position, and the dog's eyes flew open immediately.

"Sorry," she murmured, trying to calm the beast. She would have killed for something cold to drink and a trip to the bathroom.

Her eyes began to roam the room once again, taking note of the attractive, strictly masculine furnishings. When they were living together, Tyler had not been overly impressed with fine furnishings, but along with everything else, his taste had changed in that, too, she thought resentfully. The ultramodern dark corduroy furniture was accented with all-glass tables. A large bar ran the length of the room on the south side, and the entire east wall was glass. Keely could not detect one sign of a woman's touch in the room. The massive stone fireplace showed signs of a recent fire, the faint smell of smoke still clinging to the air.

Tyler had always enjoyed a fire in a fireplace, and many was the time they had made love in front of the one in their own apartment. Keely's thoughts suddenly shifted. *I wonder how many women he has made love to in this very room—in front of this very fireplace!* She struggled to pattern her thoughts in a new direction. It hurt too much to think of another woman in Tyler's arms, but no doubt there had been, because Tyler had been a very virile and insatiable man. She wouldn't allow herself to think about that. He wasn't hers any longer, so what did it matter whose arms he spent his time in?

Keely was strongly considering the possibility of making a eunuch out of her estranged husband when she finally heard the click of the key at the door. He had graciously decided to end her misery.

Her heart paused briefly as the door opened and she was at long last looking into the cool, distant eyes of Tyler Jerico. He halted for a second, his gray eyes locking with her wide blue ones. Keely sat quietly, drinking in the sight of his familiar form. The wide breadth of his shoulders, the granite firmness of his chest, the lean, slender waist, the powerful thighs and leg muscles constrained tightly in a pair of blue-gray corduroy slacks. A matching jacket was slung over his arm casually. The crisp dark blue of his tailored shirt and contrasting tie portrayed the image of a successful man. That was the key word—man. He was so breathtakingly virile standing in the dim light of the hall, Keely had to fight the overwhelming desire to go to him. Hundreds of memories came surfacing in her mind: Tyler making love to her on their honeymoon; Tyler riding his bike with her in the park on a warm summer afternoon; Tyler with his shirt off, his heavily corded muscles flexing with exertion as he had helped her move furniture in a mad weekend of frantic fall housecleaning, both of them laughing and teasing each other in happy camaraderie. Memories of Tyler making love to her in front of a warm, snapping fire on a cold winter night poured through her mind. His warm and loving kiss of gratitude as he had opened his prized gun on Christmas morning. The way he swooped her up in his arms to carry her back to their bedroom. His look of love and desire taking her breath away. Gone—all of that gone forever.

The painful look that crossed Tyler's face was, for one brief moment, so heartbreaking that Keely's heart soared. Maybe, just maybe, he still cared one small bit . . . but her hopes were dashed in the next minute as he carefully composed his expression, as if he had pulled a mask over his face. A mask she had seen too many times before.

Stepping into the apartment, he closed the door behind him, throwing the keys on a nearby table. The monstrous dog jumped to his feet and loped happily over to greet his master. "How you doing, Poochie?" Tyler greeted him affectionately.

Keely watched the man and dog jealously. So far he had greeted the dog with love, but hadn't said one word to her. "Does that dog bite?" Keely found her voice.

Cold slits of steel turned her way. "Hello, Keely."

"Tyler." Keely acknowledged his greeting with a slight nod of her head.

Tyler walked over to the bar and opened a small refrigerator. He withdrew a beer and with one smooth movement had snapped the tab off the can and deposited it into the small wastebasket sitting by the bar. "Care for something to drink?" he asked politely.

Keely's dry mouth begged for deliverance. "Yes, please."

"Beer?"

Beer, swamp water, anything! She wasn't picky. She was dying!

"Do you have a Coke?"

Tyler withdrew a red can, popped the tab, then handed her the cold drink. She accepted it greedily and brought the can up eagerly to her dry mouth. She finished the drink in a matter of seconds.

Tyler stood watching her in mild astonishment. "Damn, Kelly! Did you just come in out of the desert?"

"Very funny, Tyler. I've been held prisoner on this couch since I arrived over an hour ago," she said crossly.

Tyler stared at her in disgust. "What are you talking about?"

"The dog," she sputtered. "Why didn't you tell me you had a vicious dog in this apartment?"

"Vicious dog!" He looked at the large animal standing patiently beside him. "You're the one who's nuts! Poochie wouldn't bite a flea."

"Poochie? You mean to tell me that monstrous dog's name is *Poochie*!"

"Yes, what about it?" Tyler walked over and sat down in the chair next to the couch where she had been marooned.

Keely felt foolish. She had been cringing in her boots over a two-hundred-pound *Poochie*! "He looks dangerous," she muttered defensively.

"He's not."

Keely looked at him resentfully. "What are you doing with a dog? I didn't think you even liked them."

28

"He's not mine. I'm keeping him for a . . . friend."

The way he said it, Keely had no doubts about the gender of his "friend." Their eyes met lingeringly once again as the silence in the room grew oppressive.

"May I use your bathroom?" Keely suddenly burst out.

"What?" Tyler said, cocking one eyebrow questioningly.

Keely bit her lower lip and flushed a mild pink. Her question obviously had not been what her husband had been expecting her to say after a six-month separation. But, after all, an hour spent with a dog breathing down her neck had taken its toll on her.

"Your bathroom." Keely barely glanced at him now. "May I use your bathroom?"

Tyler shifted around in his chair, looking a little uncomfortable. "Down the hall, first door on the right." Then he bestowed a smile of condescension upon her. "Do make yourself at home, Mrs. Jerico."

With as much dignity as she could muster, Keely rose to her feet and sauntered casually out of the room. Once she was out of her overbearing husband's purview, she made a beeline for the first door on the right.

Keely delayed returning to the living room as long as possible. She stood examining herself in the large lighted mirror in the brown and beige tiled bathroom. She quickly assessed her rumpled appearance and regretted not bringing her purse along with her. She was without the small makeup case and comb she always carried. Running her fingers through her hair lightly, she tried in vain to restore a more orderly look. She peered closer into the mirror, wishing she at least had some lipstick to put on. She had chewed all hers off two hours ago.

This is silly, she scolded herself. *Why in the world am I worrying about my appearance? It's perfectly obvious he couldn't care less if I had every tooth out and never shaved my legs!* He had barely been above the level of civil since he had entered the apartment ten minutes ago. Neverthe-

29

less, Keely tried to pinch some color back in her cheeks and bit her lips to add a little rosiness before she opened the door and walked out to face her very handsome, but stubborn, adversary.

The object of her frustration was standing in front of the solid wall of glass, staring off into the distance at the mountains. The view beyond him was spectacular, the lights of the distant city twinkling merrily in the darkness. He turned at the sound of her footsteps entering the room, his cold gray appraisal showing no sign of warmth or welcome. The large great Dane walked over to her side and nuzzled gently at her hand. Keely looked at him in wry disapproval. "Why didn't you show this side of your nature hours ago . . . Poochie?" she asked sternly. His large tail wagged hesitantly, his big brown eyes pleading for understanding as she relented and patted his head.

"Did you come alone?" The sound of Tyler's voice sliced into her thoughts, bringing her back to her surroundings abruptly. Giving the dog a final pat, Keely walked back over to the couch and sat down.

"Yes, I came by myself. Dad was busy." She nervously plucked at a loose thread on her skirt. Why did she feel so uneasy around him when all she really wanted to do was throw herself in his arms and beg him to love her again. Why did she feel so vulnerable around him?

"Well, that's surprising. I would have thought Lover Boy wouldn't have let you out of his sight long enough for you to make the trip."

Keely tensed, then replied in a cool tone of voice, "Lover Boy? And who may I ask might Lover Boy be?"

A hard mask of arrogance molded his proud features as he took a drink of the Scotch he held in his hand, but his eyes plainly revealed an inner turmoil eating away at him. He lowered the glass carefully from his mouth. His back was still turned from her as he spoke. "Come on, Keely. Knock off the crap! You know perfectly well who I'm referring to. Why isn't Craig with you? Or do you have a whole string of conquests now?" His voice was sharp and unrelenting, his body tense.

Keely dug her nails into the palms of her hands, fighting to overcome the urge to pick up the ashtray lying on the coffee table in front of her and to fling it at his arrogant back. She had not seen Craig Easton since the night Tyler had walked out on her in the restaurant. She had told Craig in no uncertain terms she wanted nothing more to do with him, either personally or businesswise, after that evening. Her Dad's construction firm had lost Craig's business, but it had survived.

"Tyler!" she exploded between clenched teeth. "I have tried to tell you that there was nothing between Craig and me at any time, but if you're determined to believe there was, then so be it!"

She could see the tight muscle along the firm line of his jaw begin to work in agitation. "What the hell difference does it make now? It's over!" He walked to the bar to pour himself another drink. She never remembered him drinking more than one drink at a time during their brief marriage.

Keely felt another unwanted wave of desire wash over her as she studied his face from where she sat. She could see the deep dimple on his one cheek work enticingly as he took a long swallow of the strong liquor. She recalled the many times she had teased that dimple with the tip of her tongue, arousing him instantly. That had always been one of the secret weapons she had used on him when she wanted her way about something. He would always become putty in her hands as she gently teased and tormented him until he agreed to give her the moon. Somehow she had the strong feeling that it wouldn't work anymore. He wouldn't give her a pebble now. She blushed a bright red as she realized he was looking directly at her, his look telling her he *knew* her thoughts!

"It *is* over, isn't it, Keely?" Tyler continued in a heckling tone. "It sure didn't take you long to get here with the divorce papers. There must be someone waiting to take my place in your bed—if he hasn't already."

Keely counted to ten under her breath, then answered calmly. "If that's what you want to believe . . ." Then, smiling innocently, she added, "I have every right to—you walked out on me."

Tyler slammed the glass down on the padded bar, his face a steel mask. He strode back over to continue his perusal of the view from his window and stood staring out into the dark night for several minutes before he asked in a bleak tone, "And how many times a week do you exercise that right, my dear wife?"

"How many times do you?" she returned quietly.

He whirled back around to face her, his silver eyes snapping. "That's none of your damn business—we're not talking about me!"

Keely and the dog both came to their feet at the same moment, the dog anticipating Keely, who was boiling mad. "How dare you! You pigheaded, obstinate, hare-brained jackass! Why should my love life be any concern of yours either?"

She was standing before him now, shaking her finger under his slightly startled nose, her blue eyes shooting bolts of blue flame. "Tyler Jerico, you make me so mad, I'd like to pop you one!" she raged helplessly.

Keely was beside herself with anger. His low opinion of her hurt. She had never looked at another man, much less gone out with one, from the day she had met him. How could he treat her in such a shabby, degrading manner, as if they had never meant anything special to each other?

Tyler took a cautious step back from her, the old fire of resentment blazing brightly again in his eyes. Regaining his poise quickly, he mocked her coldly, "You're scaring me out of my wits, Keely. What are you going to do, get your powder puff out and beat me to death?"

"You'd just better thank your guardian angel I'm not a man, or I'd belt you one right now!" She hated herself for letting him get under her skin, but she still felt herself doubling up her fist and shaking it in his face to show him she meant business.

"Oh, no, you wouldn't," he sneered. "Because if you *were* a man, I would have had you laid out cold five minutes ago! And you'd better take your fist out of my face, or the fact that you're *not* a man is going to make very little difference. Do you read me loud and clear, Mrs. Jerico?"

Keely's hand dropped back to her side swiftly, but not before she bestowed him another withering glare. "You wouldn't dare," she mumbled under her breath, but didn't seem inclined to put him to the test at the moment. "You lay one hand on me, and you'll be sorry!"

"Oh, really?" He cocked his eyebrow arrogantly.

"Yes, really!" She cocked her eyebrow more arrogantly. She couldn't even imagine why they were going through this ridiculous conversation. Tyler Jerico would never lay a hand on her, and they both knew it.

They were facing each other like boxers in a ring. Poochie was standing uneasily in the middle of them now, looking from one angry face to the other. Keely broke away first, reaching frantically for her purse with the divorce papers folded neatly in it.

"You just sign these papers, Mr. Jerico, and I'll gladly be out of your life forever—that is, as soon as you buy my ticket back. I paid for my way out here and it's only fair you pay my way back."

"That couldn't be soon enough for me. Where are the damn papers?" He stormed over to stand behind her as she rummaged wildly in her disorganized purse, her face becoming pink and flushed. Darn that man! Finally, in desperation, she dumped the entire contents out on the couch. They both stood staring down at the lipstick, loose change, gum wrappers, crumpled tissues, car keys, breath mints, hairpins, combs, makeup pouch, one hair curler, and the doughnut wrapped in waxed paper that Keely had bought

33

for breakfast the day before, all of which came tumbling out.

"Jeez, Keely, that's disgusting!" he spat out nastily.

"Who asked your opinion?" she said just as nastily, handing him the rumpled papers. "Just sign these, and let's get this over with!"

Keely kept wiping discreetly at her eyes, which were threatening to fill with unwanted tears. This man was nerve-racking! Tyler was shuffling through the papers calmly, pausing occasionally to read the fine print. She began to search through the contents on the sofa, looking for a pen for him to sign with. Finding one, she thrust it at him hostilely.

"If you would just *once* control your anger and jealousy, Tyler, this day would have never come," she lectured belligerently. "Always trying to pick a fight with me. Never listening to reason!"

Tyler was looking disgustedly at the dark splotches of ink running down his fingers from the leaky ball-point she had handed him. "Me?" he laughed sarcastically, raising his eyebrows in amazement. "It's not *me* who has the temper! It's *you*!" He went back to reading the papers with interest, holding them gingerly between the only two fingertips that remained clean.

"Ha! That's a laugh if I ever heard one. I don't have a temper—" she paused, realizing that that *was* stretching the truth somewhat, but knowing full well her temper was nothing compared to his. "We can't be in a room together for five minutes without you picking a fight. Now, admit it!"

Tyler glanced back up at her in defiance. "I will not admit any such thing! You're the pigheaded one in this marriage, not me."

"Oh, really?" She was doing a slow burn again.

"Yes, really," he sneered sweetly.

"You just wouldn't want to make a little bet on that, would you?"

Tyler looked at his wife's flushed, angry, but determined face. "Such as?" he asked, picking up the gauntlet.

"Such as . . ." Keely thought for a moment. This argument was beginning to get out of hand. "Such as, I'll bet you ten dollars that you couldn't spend two hours in the same room with me without *you* starting a fight." There! She had him. If he was honest, he would have to admit that he couldn't.

He stared at her as if she had become totally deranged. "Wow—ten dollars! No way. I couldn't take your money like that. Forget it, Keely, I'm too much of a gentleman to take that much money from a woman," he said sarcastically. "Besides, anyone could stay in the same room with someone for two hours without a fight. Why don't you up the odds?" He leaned back on the small bar and crossed his arms negligently, a cocky grin spreading across his face.

Keely peered at his handsome features, her pulse racing. "What did you have in mind?" she asked cautiously.

"Well, let's at least make it interesting, Big Mouth."

Keely gritted her teeth. "How interesting, Pain in the Rear?"

Tyler's cocky grin faded at her unfortunate choice of words. "All right, Hothead, I'll bet you a thousand dollars." He paused for a second, a devious smile crossing his face. "No wait, I'll bet you all our community property. That should make it easier on both of us—a clear-cut divorce—winner take all—I'll bet you that you can't live here with me for one week without *you* losing your temper." He was safe. She would never be able to do that, and she knew it!

"Is that right? Well, let me tell you this, you horse's rear, I not only accept that challenge, I welcome it—if you can live with me without losing *your* temper. I'd be more than happy to prove to you and the world that it isn't my fault our marriage didn't work. It's because you simply are an ill-tempered man whom *no* one could live with!" Keely's heart was racing at full speed. What was she doing? If she lost this ridiculous bet, she would be financially ruined! He would have her furniture, car—everything!

Tyler's smile left his face permanently this time as the meaning of her words hit him. "You mean you're accepting the bet?" he asked, amazed.

Keely smiled shakily. She wouldn't back out now. She would just have to make darn sure she won the bet! "I'm accepting the bet!"

Tyler shook his head. "Look, Keely, you'd better reconsider. There's a lot at stake here."

"Second thoughts, Tyler?" she taunted.

"No, I just hate to leave a woman out in the cold. It would be like taking candy from a baby."

"I wouldn't count on that, but if you don't want to go ahead with the bet, I'll understand." She looked smugly victorious as she began to stuff everything back into her purse hurriedly, praying he would back out. "Just sign the papers, give me the money for my return ticket, and I'll be on my way," she said airily.

Tyler laid the unsigned papers down on the coffee table, his face a cool mask of indifference. "Oh, I'm accepting the bet, Keely. I just don't want you crying foul at the end of the week when you're left with nothing."

Keely straightened up, her heart sinking as the full implication of their impulsive bet hit her. Was she nuts? She had just put everything she owned on the line—plus trapped herself into spending a full week here with Tyler! The enormity of the situation hit her, causing her knees to go weak. She sank down helplessly on the sofa. "Now, wait a minute, Tyler . . ."

"No! You agreed to the bet. Now you'll have to live with it."

Keely swallowed hard. "But I don't want to live here as your . . . wife!"

A sadistic grin slowly spread across Tyler's face.

"What's the matter, Keely, have you forgotten how to . . . cook?"

"Cook? No, that wasn't what I was thinking of, Tyler."

"I know what you were thinking, and that's entirely up to you whether you want me to be your 'husband' for a week or not. I'm game. We never had any trouble in that area."

Keely sprang up in self-defense. "Whether or not *I* want *you* to be my husband!" she said indignantly. "If you think I came out here to sleep with you for a week, then turn around and go back home and get a divorce, you're crazy! How dare you—you inconsiderate son-of-a—"

"All right. Forget it, Keely. The bet doesn't include bedroom privileges." He looked at her and grinned. "I'll continue to find my entertainment outside the home. All I'll ask of you is your culinary arts."

"Well, I never . . ."

"You're right—not with me, unless you beg!" His grin widened.

"Beg! I wouldn't go to bed with you if you were the last man on earth," she assured him huffily, "and it disgusts me to no end to think *you* would think that *I* would even suggest such a thing!"

"Just so we understand each other, honey," he said calmly. He glanced down at his watch, then back at her. "Okay, starting right now, for one week, you live in harmony with me. If you lose, you're out in the cold, baby, and I don't want to hear you whimpering about it."

"Tyler!" she blurted.

"You better smile when you say my name like that from now on, sweetheart."

Keely pasted a plastic smile on her face. "What I was going to say, *darling*, was, I feel that we should have gotten a few more things clear. Such as, where *will* I sleep?"

"Fall straight back and you're in bed," Tyler said helpfully.

Keely turned around and looked at the sofa. "You mean I'm sleeping here?"

"There's only one bed in this apartment and *I* sleep in it. If you're not sleeping with me—"

"But, I thought you would be the gentleman and give *me* the bedroom and you take the sofa," she smiled sweetly.

"Not on your life. That sofa looks pretty, but it's as uncomfortable as hell to sleep on!"

Keely bit back her response, determined to make the best of the ridiculous situation. "Thanks for telling me."

"No problem. By the end of the week you'll be praying for mercy," he assured her. "Well, I'm hungry. How about you?"

"Yes, I am getting hungry." Ha! Who was she kidding? She was starved!

"Well, since you're the guest, I'll let you pick what we eat tonight. What sounds good to you?" he offered in a rare show of generosity.

Keely thought for a moment, then her eyes lit up. "Pizza."

Tyler whirled away from the window where he had been standing again. "Pizza! I *hate* . . ." He caught himself just in time. "You know I don't like pizza, darling. How about something else?"

"No," Keely said, thinking for a moment, her blue eyes very innocent as she turned them back on him. "I seem to be craving pizza tonight. With lots of anchovies!"

Tyler's face turned a shade paler. "Anchovies?" he muttered weakly.

"Yes, please. Tell them to load it down with anchovies —and, Tyler, while you're gone, I think I'll just take a nice hot bath and relax for a while." Keely began to gather her small suitcase and handbag together, heading for the bathroom she had been in earlier. "Oh, and by the way, I want a large one."

Tyler was putting his suit jacket on when he stopped in

midair, staring at her incredulously. "Hell . . . uh, darling, the closest pizza parlor is twenty miles from here."

"Really? How inconvenient! But that gives me plenty of time for a long leisurely bath." She winked deviously. "Hurry back, I'll miss you!"

CHAPTER THREE

Keely opened one eye droopily. What was that sound? She listened attentively, turning her head sideways. Her cornflower blue eyes stared into large chocolate-colored ones intently. Dawn was barely streaking through the sheer curtains hanging at the windows. Keely heard the sound again—a whining, pitiful sound coming from Poochie's throat.

"What's the matter, Poochie? Do you need to go outside?" Keely mumbled sleepily.

The whining sounded more serious now as the dog edged even closer to the sofa, his head nuzzling for her hand.

"All right, come on." She threw the blanket back and stepped out onto the cold floor. Darn, it's freezing in this room this morning, she thought miserably as she hurried over to let the dog out the back door. A cold gust of frigid wind whipped around the tail of her skimpy nightgown as the dog bounded around her out into the brisk early morning air. Keely stood for a moment drinking in the glorious scene before her. Pikes Peak loomed in the distance, its snowcapped peak reaching toward the heavens.

Another gust of wind forced Keely to slam the door and

fly back to the sofa in a running bound. She snuggled back under the warm blanket, her body a mass of soreness. She felt as though she had slept on a railroad tie. Tyler had been generous in describing the sofa as merely "uncomfortable." She had never spent a more miserable night in her entire life! How could anything look so beautiful, yet be so torturous? She had tossed and turned the better part of the night, finally managing to drop off into a fitful slumber in the wee hours of the morning. She didn't feel as though she had been asleep over thirty minutes before the dog had summoned her attention. Keely simmered at the thought that Tyler had made her sleep out here in the first place! Then to put the responsibility of the dog in her hands was just too much! As they were getting ready for bed last night, Tyler had informed her that the dog would sleep out here with her. He said since he was such a sound sleeper, he was afraid he wouldn't be able to hear the dog, so would she mind seeing that he was let out for his morning duties? He had shut his bedroom door in her face before she had had time to protest, which she couldn't have done anyway.

She grinned secretly to herself as she snuggled down more warmly on the uncomfortable sofa. He was only paying her back for making him take that long trip for pizza last night. Her smile widened as she thought of his driving twenty miles for a pizza she didn't eat. He had returned three hours later, carrying a cold, soggy pizza and soaking wet. A fine mist had started falling around ten o'clock, making the cold fall night wet and miserable. He had told her in a tight voice that he was sorry he was so late, but he had had a flat when he came out of the pizza parlor, and his spare was flat also. It had taken him an hour and a half to find a service station that would fix flats at that time of night. Keely had assured him in one of her sweetest voices that it was perfectly all right, she had decided to fix herself a peanut butter sandwich not long after he left, realizing she was too hungry to wait for the

41

pizza. If looks could have killed, they would have been putting Keely away this morning, but the voice that came out of the stony face was mild. "Then I guess we won't be needing this sickening mess, will we?" And he opened the trash can and dropped the pizza box in it ceremoniously.

Well, that *was* a dirty trick to play on him, she knew, but it was imperative that she win this bet. If she could make him mad today, she could be on a plane by this evening, divorce papers in hand. He had held up well last night, but she knew her Tyler. He'd never make it through today!

She was just beginning to doze off in a warm, fuzzy cocoon, when she heard the scratching on the back door. With a deep groan she staggered back out of the bed and walked over to the door again. An exuberant, wide-awake Poochie nearly knocked her down to return to the warmth and comfort of the house. He began licking her hand, telling her he was now ready for his breakfast, in his eagerness, nearly knocking her off her feet.

"Oh, come on, Poochie. It's too early to eat yet," she pleaded, glancing up at the clock on the mantel. "Good heavens! Seven o'clock!" But the dog obviously couldn't tell time, and his stomach told him it was morning. With a sigh of resignation Keely followed the dog into the kitchen. She turned on the light and marveled again at the loveliness of this room. Sunny yellow appliances gleamed bright and clean in the early morning light. Shiny pots and pans hung above a butcher-block bar that ran down the length of the kitchen. The whole south wall in here was composed of windows looking out on the treetops that covered the hillside. The brilliant colors of fall shone brightly, casting a warm glow over the room. A glass table with four swivel chairs brightly upholstered in a sunny yellow sat in front of the gleaming windows, while a small eating bar with four wicker stools graced the other half of the kitchen. Keely had never seen a more beautiful room, in fact, a more beautiful apartment, than this one. Tyler certainly had good taste. She began searching for the dog food, finding a monstrous sack sitting inside the small utility room beside a matching yellow washer and dryer.

After dumping out a gigantic amount of the dry food, she sat the bowl down in front of the dog and jerked her hand back rapidly as Poochie began to inhale the contents of the bowl. Walking back over to the island bar, she spied a coffeepot, which she promptly put to use. She was wide awake now, so there was no point going back to that uncomfortable sofa. She would just sit in here and read the paper and drink coffee before Tyler got up. Then she would fix breakfast for both of them. She was surprised as she realized she was actually looking forward to cooking his meals this week! She had always loved to cook for him because he had enjoyed anything she had put on the table. With the one exception of pizza. He had always hated pizza—the mere thought of it turned his stomach.

A pot of coffee and two hours later, Tyler walked into the kitchen, his eyes still drowsy with sleep. The short terry-cloth robe he was wearing was open to his waist, revealing a broad expanse of his very hairy, sexy chest. Keely swallowed hard and dropped her eyes back down to the magazine she had been reading, trying to keep her eyes off his legs, which had the same thick coating of dark hair that covered his chest. The recipe for the tuna casserole that had looked so good earlier now paled to insignificance as Tyler reached for a cup and poured himself some coffee.

"How was your night?" he asked nonchalantly as he took the chair opposite her, running his fingers through the thick, wiry hair on his head.

"Short," she said disinterestedly as she went back to scanning the pages of her magazine.

"Did you sleep well?" A small grin was playing across his unshaven face.

Keely met his arrogant eyes with the cool blue of hers. "Yes, thank you."

He chuckled knowingly and picked up a section of the morning paper. "What's for breakfast?"

"I noticed you have a waffle iron. Would you like some waffles and sausage?" she asked pleasantly, turning the pages of her magazine faster.

"Sounds good to me. I'm hungry." He took another sip of his coffee, his eyes scanning the sports page.

Keely rose to her feet and began assembling the ingredients for the waffles, neither one of them trying to carry on a conversation. Within fifteen minutes Keely set a plate of delectable golden brown waffles with link sausages before him. Handing him the pitcher of warm maple syrup, she sat down across from him and eagerly began to eat hers.

Tyler laid the paper down and casually picked up his fork and began eating. He had cleaned his plate in five minutes and went back to his paper without saying a word to her.

She was savoring the rich sweet taste of the maple syrup, her mind wandering in all directions, when he finally spoke from behind his paper. "If you think you'll have any spare money left after you lose the bet," he said in a pleasant tone, "there's a big sale going on right now." He moved the paper a bit so he could see her face as he commented. "It says here they have all sizes in their winter clothes, ranging from fives to"—he casually looked her up and down with his cool gray eyes—"the *larger* sizes on sale today."

Keely's fork paused in midair as she was about to take another bite of her sausage. "What do you mean by *larger* sizes?" she asked in a controlled voice.

"Oh, I didn't mean to imply you would need a larger size," he hastened to add, "although I have noticed you've put on a few pounds since I last saw you." He went back to reading the paper.

Keely looked down at her body, her eyes growing puzzled. "A few pounds? I haven't gained any weight, Tyler!"

He lowered the paper once again, his eyes assessing her

once more. "Really?" The tone of his voice indicated he didn't believe her.

Keely laid her fork down and pushed back her half-eaten plate of food. What was he talking about? She hadn't gained any weight—well, maybe a couple of pounds, but, good heavens, who didn't gain a couple of pounds once in a while. She sipped at her coffee, trying not to let his remark get under her skin.

"What size do you think I wear, Tyler?" she finally blurted out, unable to control her curiosity any longer.

Tyler glanced up from the paper, his face a perfect mask of innocence. "Now, if you think I'm going to answer that loaded question, you can think again. I wouldn't touch that with a ten-foot pole!"

"No, really," she said, encouraging him to answer. "I won't get mad. What size do you think I wear?" She could bite her tongue off. She knew full well she was asking for trouble, but she seemed powerless to stop herself.

"No way, Keely," Tyler said firmly. "I've never tried to talk to women about their figures—or lack of them," he said pointedly.

Keely would have liked to knock his block off, but, instead, she sat quietly drinking her coffee. It was obviously one of his tricks to try to irritate her. Well, the joke was on him, because she wouldn't fall for it.

A few moments elapsed before Tyler's deep voice came from behind the paper. "Just as a matter of curiosity, Keely, what size *would* a slightly chunky woman wear?" he asked with interest.

"I wouldn't know, Tyler," Keely said through gritted teeth, fighting the overwhelming urge to kick him out of his chair. The very nerve of him insulting her in that nice tone of voice!

"Well, just take a guess," he persisted. "Say the woman's about five feet two, not much in the chest department, waist a little thick, legs a tiny bit flabby, but not too bad for her age. What would you say? Sixteen? Eight—"

45

"Do you *know* someone with that problem, Tyler," she cut in menacingly, "or are you just making conversation?" Keely was beginning to steam.

"No, I know someone like that," he assured her readily. "I thought I'd buy her a present. Something from the big sale today."

Keely shoved away from the table and stalked over to the sink. If she sat at the table with him five more minutes, she *would* be flat broke!

"Ask the saleslady at the department store. I don't know about the larger sizes. *I* wear an *eight,*" she stressed, running water into the sink.

"Ah, well," he sighed, folding the paper back up neatly and placing it beside his plate. "It was probably a bad idea anyway. She would appreciate a book more than clothes. I imagine it would be rather depressing to have to wear the larger sizes, although she has a lovely face." He stood up from the table, stretching. "Well, time to start the old grind. Can you find plenty to do to keep yourself busy today?"

"I'm sure I can." Keely was busy washing the skillet she had cooked the sausage links in. "Everything looks nice and clean. Do you do your own housekeeping?"

"Nope. I have a woman come in twice a week. By the way, I'll call her and give her the week off. You don't mind keeping things straight, do you? Give you something to do with your time."

"I hadn't planned on being a domestic when I made the trip," she reminded him, but in a polite tone of voice.

"There's very little to be done around here. Just the usual straightening up, and, if I remember correctly, you do like a clean house."

"That's right." Keely was still scrubbing the skillet. If there was one thing that got under her skin, it was a messy house. But there would be no problems there. Tyler had never been messy. He was neat and tidy—for a man.

"Don't worry about dinner tonight. I'll bring something home from the store. Save you a shopping trip."

"That's fine with me. I'll just clean up around here, then relax this afternoon." She dried the skillet and replaced it in the cabinet.

As Keely straightened the living room and folded her sheets and blankets, she heard the sounds of Tyler getting ready for work. How good it felt once again to have breakfast with him, then tidy up his house. Of course, this wasn't the house they had lived in together, but there were still unmistakable signs of Tyler flooding the apartment. The black powder muzzle loader that she had given him last Christmas was hanging in a prominent place over the fireplace. One of his shirts was draped over the back of a chair, smelling faintly of the musky aftershave he always wore. His keys and billfold were lying on the small hall table, where he had thrown them last night. Small signs to say a man lived here. A very virile and handsome man, one who any woman would be proud to call her own. If he had only loved her enough to trust her, this could very well be her home, because they had talked often of coming back to Colorado so he could start his own construction firm. But he *hadn't* loved her enough to trust her, and after this week, the marriage would definitely be over.

Tyler appeared at the door, his clean smell wafting out into the room. Keely's pulse fluttered as she watched him finish buttoning his pale blue shirt. A pair of dark charcoal slacks fit him snugly, showing the hard-muscled smoothness of his thighs and legs. He was carrying a matching jacket in his other hand as he walked across the room toward the front door.

"I should be home around six," he was saying, his hands working unsuccessfully with the stubborn tie. He cursed softly under his breath after two disastrous tries at tying it to his satisfaction. Looking at her helplessly, he asked, "Can you do something with this damn thing?"

Keely dropped the blanket she was folding and walked

over to take the tie in her hands. Her knees suddenly weakened as her closeness to him invaded her senses. Her hands trembled slightly as she worked, seemingly effortlessly, with the tie, tying a perfect knot, as she had done so many times before for him. She could smell his aftershave as she closed her eyes painfully to blot out the old memories. Her eyes opened slowly to lock for just a fraction of a second with his, both of them glancing away as quickly as possible. Neither spoke a word. Keely would have never found her voice if he had said anything to her at that moment. A large lump seemed to block her air passage as they stood facing each other in the quiet room, Keely gently adjusting the dark gray tie with the lighter gray stripe running through it.

Their eyes met once again; this time neither one found the courage to break the gaze. Keely began to drown in the deep silver of his eyes, remembering the times when she had lain in his arms, reveling in their love for each other. It wasn't that long ago, yet it was a lifetime.

"There," she whispered, softly patting the tie into place. "One perfect knot."

His eyes were still holding hers, his hands now coming out to gently encircle her waist, drawing her closer to the lean hardness of his body as he had done so many times before. "I've missed you, Keely." His voice was as smooth, deep, and rich as dark velvet; his hands moved restlessly along the side of her rib cage, stopping just below the fullness of her breasts.

"Have you?" she whispered back in a shaky voice, her hands moving up now to his broad shoulders, smoothing the rough texture of his suit, her fingers moving in a nervous manner.

"Of course, I have. We had our good times." His face was very near to hers, yet he made no move to close the distance.

"Yes," she responded softly. "We did."

Their eyes were searching each other's faces now, each

one seeking out the other's familiar planes and angles. It was growing increasingly harder for Keely to draw a clear breath of air standing here in Tyler's arms. She wanted him to kiss her so badly. She was disturbed at the intensity of that feeling. She wanted once again to experience one of those deep, mind-drugging kisses that seemed to go on forever in the dark of the night—to feel his warm lips on hers—and she didn't want it to end there. She wanted to be made love to, one more time. At this moment she wanted all of Tyler Jerico.

It must have been written in her eyes, the desire and longing she felt for him, because he suddenly pushed her gently away, but not before she felt the trembling in his own body, assuring her he had not gone totally untouched by the intimate scene that had just taken place.

"Thanks for the help, Keely." He had turned back to the cold and indifferent Tyler whom she had known so well. "I'll see you tonight."

He opened the door and was gone, swiftly leaving a trembling twenty-seven-year-old woman standing alone in the quiet room, tears sliding down her face.

She managed to bring herself under control and went to the bathroom to wash her face with cold water. She stepped into the room and nearly jumped back from shock. It looked as if a cyclone had come through it. Tyler's robe, towel, and washrag were thrown on the floor. Water was splashed all over the floor, and he had apparently cleaned his razor out in the sink, the nasty dark bristles stuck to it in a disgusting manner. The mirror in front of the sink looked like someone had stood back and literally spat toothpaste, as they might tobacco, at it. The tops were off the toothpaste, his aftershave, the mouthwash, and a new bar of soap had been opened and the wrapper thrown on the floor. How one man could have destroyed this room with the speed that he had was truly amazing.

Keely set about to straighten "the remains," working

for a full hour. She was fuming again as she finished the job, feeling certain he had deliberately destroyed the room to irritate her. He had always been neat when they lived together, with the exception of one room that he reserved for his private things. It had always been a disorganized mess, but he would scream to high heaven if Keely ever tried to straighten up or tamper with it. That was *his* private domain, and he wanted things left untouched. Keely grinned devilishly to herself as she wiped the last of the toothpaste from the mirror. If he had one of those rooms then, he undoubtedly would have one now!

Throwing down the paper towels and Windex, she set out to explore the remainder of the apartment. It didn't take her long to find what she was looking for. The second door she opened off the hall revealed what she had hoped to find. It was also in the order she had expected. Tyler had centered everything of special interest to him in this room. Guns, books, a machine to reload shells, bows, arrows, fishing equipment, heads of trophy deer, elk, and moose, large mounted fish—all lined the walls. Stacks of magazines turned to certain sections and left open for future reference lay on the tables. He had been tying his own flies for trout fishing, all of the material carefully laid out before the chair where he obviously did his work. The room was in a disorganized shambles, just as he wanted it.

Keely set about her task, reaching for the Pledge and dusting cloth, and for the rest of the day worked at a fever pitch. At the end of the day she stood in the doorway, proudly surveying the sparkling interior. It now fit the rest of the apartment. Everything was neat and orderly. All the books lay resting in a magazine rack, all the material for his lures lay in a drawer. Everything was perfect. Tyler would be surprised—to say the least!

She just had time to make the phone call to her dad before Tyler got home, which she had been putting off all day. Devin had seemed a little surprised, but not overly concerned, when Keely had told him she wouldn't be returning home for a few days. Of course, she hadn't told him why she had been delayed; she simply implied that Tyler was being a little obstinate about signing the divorce papers. Promising to keep in touch, she had hung up the phone and had taken a long, leisurely bath. She put on her clean pair of jeans, wondering what she was going to do about her clothes. If she didn't get Tyler to lose his temper soon, she would have to stay longer than planned, and would need more than a couple of changes of clothes.

A little after six she heard the key in the front door. She replaced the fingernail file in her purse and went to meet him at the door. She hoped he had brought something good to eat; she was starved. Amidst all the cleaning today, she had forgotten to eat lunch.

"Hi," she greeted him as he walked in the door and put down the large sack he had in his hand.

"Hi. You getting hungry?"

"Starved. How about you?"

"I could certainly eat." He walked over and gave Poochie an exuberant greeting. The dog had dutifully followed Keely around the apartment all day as she had cleaned.

"I'll just get things started. Why don't you sit down and just relax," Keely said pleasantly. "I'll only be a minute."

"Thanks. I am tired. I've been in meetings all day." He loosened his tie and sank down gratefully in one of the corduroy chairs.

"How long do you have to watch Poochie?" she called on the way to the kitchen. It wasn't that she didn't like the dog, she just didn't care to have one that size in the house with her all day.

"Sheila should be back by tomorrow," came the tired answer from the direction where Tyler was sitting.

Sheila? Where had she heard that name before? Oh, yes, Sheila was Tyler's secretary. So she was the dog's owner. Keely began to unload the grocery sack, taking out eggs, potatoes, cauliflower, and a big package wrapped in white

51

butcher's paper. She sure hoped it was a sixteen-ounce sirloin steak. She was so hungry she could eat a horse!

I wonder what else Sheila is to Tyler, she mused as she wrapped the potatoes in foil and stuck them in the oven. She must be more than a friend for Tyler ever to keep her dog for her. He hated dogs in the house!

She walked back over to the kitchen door and yelled in to Tyler, "Should you start the charcoal grill for this meat?"

"I don't think that will be necessary," came his bored reply, "just throw it in the skillet on the stove."

Keely shrugged her shoulders and returned to the meat. She liked her steaks cooked on an outdoor grill. She unwrapped the white package, humming under her breath. Suddenly her stomach did a flip-flop. Lying on the white paper was a hideous mass of . . . something . . . something so nauseating she nearly ran for the bathroom. Forcing herself to examine the meat more fully, she peered at the ugly blob. It looked like something out of a science-fiction movie staring back at her. Still unable to identify the contents of the package, she rewrapped the entire bundle and sauntered casually back to the kitchen door. This had to be another one of his little schemes to make her mad. "Ty," she purred, "what kind of meat is that, darling? I don't believe I've ever cooked any of . . . that . . . before."

"Brains."

"Beg your pardon?"

"Brains." His head popped up over the chair, and he smiled refreshingly. "I was sitting in one of my meetings today, and all of a sudden I had the overwhelming *urge* to have brains and eggs for supper."

Keely felt sick to her stomach. Brains! She would gag to death before she ever got them fixed!

Laughing shakily, she gripped the side of the doorjamb unsteadily. "Say you're kidding, Tyler, please."

He was on his feet, heading for the kitchen door, a pleased smirk on his face. "Would I kid about a thing like that?" He patted her head affectionately, just like he did Poochie. "How soon before we eat? I'm starved."

Keely's heart sank as she realized she was going to have to cook that obnoxious mess lying on the kitchen counter. This was going to be a tough night to get through, she could see right now. "It may take me a while, Tyler. Why don't you just go in your little den and relax awhile."

"My little den? You been exploring today?"

"Oh, just sort of doing a few little odd jobs around the house. Some I'm sure your housekeeper wouldn't want to be bothered with."

Tyler looked at her warily, realization beginning to dawn on his face. "I hope you didn't go to a lot of trouble," he stressed, hoping he was reading her wrong. "I take care of that room myself."

"Not for the next week you don't, darling," she said, smiling reassuringly. "As long as I'm here, I wouldn't dream of letting you go through all that trouble."

Tyler's face turned a sickly gray as he realized what lay before him in the other room. "You didn't really clean that room up, did you, Keely?" he asked pitifully.

"Guess." Keely smiled brightly.

"Oh, damn," he muttered tightly.

"What did you say, darling?"

"Ham! I forgot to get ham at the store."

"Oh, I thought you said something else. Well, if you'll excuse me, I'll just see about dinner."

Keely left Tyler standing in the doorway, his face clearly showing the battle that was raging within him. He finally summoned up enough nerve to jam his hands into his pants pockets and amble off slowly in the direction of his den, leaving Keely alone with the unsavory mass on the kitchen counter and a dozen eggs.

53

CHAPTER FOUR

"Tyler, your brains are fried!" Keely glanced down at the plate she was holding, and shrugged her shoulders. She didn't know any other way to describe the unappetizing fare before her. She certainly wouldn't want to commit a disservice by calling it dinner.

She sat down at the glass table and stared at her plate morosely. Tyler had an uncanny knack of putting her in a surly mood. He had been suspiciously quiet in the next room, with only an occasional groan or a muffled expletive coming from the direction of his den as she had finished preparing their meal. It wouldn't be long now before he went over the brink, she consoled herself, picking up her fork and pushing the eggs around on her plate. Then she would go home and put him out of her mind forever. Curse the day anyone so much as mentioned his name in her presence!

Tyler ambled into the kitchen and took the chair opposite her. He seemed to be holding up amazingly well for a man whose mind had obviously undergone such a traumatic shock, Keely mused, as she got up to pour him a cup of coffee.

"Your den sure looks nice, doesn't it?" she asked. "I'll bet you've found things you didn't even know you had."

"I'll bet I won't find things I *knew* I had," he answered in a clipped way, with just a touch of anger seeping through his voice. He stared bleakly at his plate. "So this is what brains look like after they're cooked. I should have stayed with my original thought of liver and cauliflower," he said glumly.

"Ummm! That sounds delicious too! Maybe we'll have that tomorrow night," she agreed cheerfully. *Lord, please let him break soon,* she pleaded mutely as she took a drink of her coffee, trying to ignore what was on her plate.

"Where's my stuffed albino squirrel?"

"What's an albino squirrel?"

"It's an unusual species of squirrel that I came across on my last hunting trip. Where did you put it?"

"I don't know," she answered a bit defensively. "Where was it lying?"

"In the corner by my gun rack," he said curtly, his gray eyes simmering. "What did you do with it?"

"Is *that* what that thing was? I thought it was something that had crawled up and died. I'm sorry, I threw it away." She nonchalantly took another sip of her coffee. This was it! He'd blow for sure.

Tyler's tanned complexion turned to a shade of ash gray. "You threw my albino squirrel away?" he managed to choke out between clinched teeth.

She glanced up innocently. "Yes, I put it in the incinerator. Does that upset you?"

Tyler's glare pinned her to her seat. "A little!"

Keely pressed onward. "If it makes you feel any better, I didn't touch another thing of yours. Well, nothing except . . ."

Her voice left him the opportunity to ask in a taut voice, "Except?"

"I did use your little silver hammer to crack some walnuts."

55

"My little silver hammer? I don't have a little silver hammer!"

"Yes, you do," she insisted. "It's lying up there next to all of the bullets you've reloaded."

"Next to my bull . . . oh, hell, Keely! You surely didn't use my custom-made, forty-four-caliber bullet mold with four cavities to crack your damn walnuts, did you?" he asked pitifully.

"Was it lying next to the bullets you reloaded?"

"Yes," he murmured weakly.

"That's the one I used then." She was beginning to get a little uneasy. This wasn't going quite like she had expected. In the past, if she had committed such an outrageous act, even innocently, he would have hit the ceiling! But the man sitting across from her was controlling his temper in a most admirable manner. She could see that tense muscle working along his jawline, and he was quietly strangling his coffee cup, yet he said nothing.

"I needed the nuts to put in the chocolate icing," she explained. "I made that cake you used to like so well. . . ." She was really beginning to feel rather sorry for him. He looked so shattered. If she had had any idea that his squirrel had been an unusual one, she would have found some other way to irritate him.

Tyler sighed, then pushed back his untouched plate. "Why don't we have dessert and forget the meal. It's been a long time since I've had a piece of your cake."

Keely felt a surge of irritation shoot through her. Hell's bells! Why did he have to be so nice about it. Now she felt like a heel.

She cut the cake in silence, handing him an extra-large serving. Her heart lightened somewhat when she saw the way he eagerly began to eat the rich chocolate confection. He had lost weight since she had last seen him and there were tired lines around his eyes now. His familiar features, which she loved so much, tugged at her heart, and she forced herself to look down at her plate, berating herself for still having such strong feelings for him, for having feelings about him at all. Because of their similar temperaments, they would never have been able to make a go of their marriage, and it was extremely fortunate that they had both realized their mistake and taken steps to end the troubled union. Someday they would both meet someone they could live in harmony with. Keely frowned as the name "Sheila" surfaced to her mind. Perhaps Tyler had already met his "someone."

"This is good," he complimented her between mouthfuls. "I've missed your cooking."

Keely stabbed her cake viciously. How romantic! He's missed my cooking! "Thank you," she muttered politely. "You look like you've lost weight. Have you been ill?"

His fork paused in midair, visions of the past clouding his eyes. "No, not ill. I just haven't had the appetite I used to have. I notice your figure hasn't suffered any."

Keely grinned at him with a friendly smile. "That's not what you said this morning. I believe you implied that I was growing matronly?"

A devilish look came into his eyes. "Who, me?"

She couldn't help laughing out loud. "Yes, you!"

His eyes caressed her softness as he spoke quietly, "Don't believe everything you hear, lovely lady. There's nothing wrong with your figure."

Her heart took a perilous leap, and she fought to ignore the familiar ache she felt for him. An ache that only he could satisfy.

"I bet you say that to all the girls," she scolded him in a coy tone.

"You're right. I do," he agreed.

Horse's rear! she thought in mutiny as she sprang to her feet and snatched his plate up.

"Hey, wait a minute, I wasn't through yet!" he protested in an amused tone.

"Yes, you are," she said firmly as she dumped the last of his cake in the garbage disposal.

"Well, if you insist," he said, grinning infectiously. "By the way, you won't mind taking care of the dog again, will you. Sheila is back in town, but we have some business to take care of tonight. I told her she was welcome to leave the dog over here until we get through."

In a defensive gesture, Keely folded her arms across her chest. "Why, heavens, no. I wouldn't care, Tyler!" She pressed her lips together in anger. "I haven't anything to do!"

Tyler looked angelic. "Does this upset you, darling?"

"Not at all, sweetheart, have a nice time." *You nerd,* she added silently.

The peal of the doorbell broke their combative gaze as Tyler gave her a mock salute and started for the front door. "If it'll make you feel any better, darling, you have my permission to scream, get mad, throw things . . ." he taunted her as he walked out of the room.

Keely flattened her palms out on the cabinet in front of her and took long, deep breaths. She would not scream! She simply would not!

The sound of a laughing voice floated into the kitchen as Keely tried to pull herself together. The voice sounded bright, cheerful, and thoroughly feminine. Regaining some semblance of control, Keely reached up to straighten her hair, then walked into the living room. The smell of Charles of the Ritz perfume tantalized the air in a faint, pleasing manner. A swift stab of jealousy pierced through Keely as she watched Tyler help Sheila off with her coat. They seemed to have an ease, a certain familiarity with each other that disturbed Keely more than she cared to admit. When she had accepted the bet with Tyler, she hadn't realized exactly what this week would entail. She had never once stopped to think that she would be exposed to Tyler's new life and all the hurt that it could hold for her. For the first time since this farce began, Keely realized with sudden clarity that even if she won, it would not be worth the pain of seeing him with another woman.

Keely glanced up and saw Sheila standing in the kitchen doorway, a beautiful smile lighting her face as she stepped forward to meet Keely. "This must be Keely," she said in a friendly greeting, extending a perfectly manicured hand. "I'm so happy to meet you at last."

Tyler came around the sofa to stand next to Keely, placing his arm around his wife's waist in a casual gesture. "Yes, Sheila, this is my wife, Keely; Keely, this is Sheila Morgan."

"How do you do," Keely said, accepting her hand graciously, wondering about Sheila's last name being the same as Chris's. "Very nice to meet you. I understand you're Tyler's secretary?"

"Tyler's and my brother Chris's. Between the two of them, I'm kept busier than I like to think about," she said, casting a playful look in Tyler's direction.

"I haven't seen anything to indicate you couldn't handle the job," Tyler grinned affectionately. "I don't know what I'd do without you, Sheila."

Keely felt a little nauseated. She was not so much concerned with what he would do *without* Sheila, it was what he was doing *with* Sheila that had her stomach in knots!

Poochie came bounding through the kitchen door, apparently just hearing the voice of his mistress. He lunged toward Sheila, and his large tongue lapped at her face with unconcealed affection. Keely had the childish thought that Tyler might very well have greeted Sheila in the same fashion if he hadn't been stuck with an ex-wife in his house!

"Poochie!" Sheila scolded as she tried to disentangle herself from the dog's amorous advances. "What am I going to do with you!"

Tyler laughed as he grabbed Poochie's collar and dragged him off Sheila. "I think he's trying to tell you he's missed you."

"And I missed him too," Sheila cooed, reaching down

lovingly to stroke the dog's lustrous fur. "Did you really miss your mama?"

"I did tell you Poochie was Sheila's dog, didn't I, Keely?" Tyler asked, glancing up at her.

Only three or four times, Keely thought resentfully. "Yes, I believe you did mention that."

"Yes, ole Poochie is Sheila's big baby," Tyler said, smiling and patting the dog again.

"I noticed the resemblance," Keely said under her breath.

Tyler glanced up. "Did you say something?"

"No, no, I was just talking to myself."

"Well, Poochie, you're going to have to let me go, or Tyler and I will be late."

Keely noticed Sheila had not mentioned what they were going to be late for.

"Give me a minute, Sheila, and I'll be right with you." Tyler left the room with Keely trailing along behind him. She did not feel like entertaining Tyler's . . . friend.

Tyler stepped into the small bath off his bedroom as Keely walked over and stood in front of the large mirror on his dresser. The sound of his electric razor broke the quietness in the room as Keely stared back at her reflection in the glass. Her hand reached up to touch the thick mane of hair that hung heavily down her back. *Such an old-fashioned style,* she thought. A picture of Sheila's ultrashort fashionable hairstyle surfaced in her mind. No wonder Tyler was attracted to her. She looked as if she had just stepped out of the pages of *Vogue* magazine. One of Kelly's fingers reached absently for one of her dark locks, wrapping it tightly around her hand. Those unwanted memories rushed back over her as she remembered the times when Tyler's hands had wound themselves in the thickness of her hair as he made love to her. When he had been in a particularly playful mood, he had bound their nude bodies together with her long hair, telling her he would never let her go, that she was his captive for life!

Such foolish words. There had been times when she had considered cutting her hair, wanting to change to an easier, more stylish cut, but he had always protested adamantly, calling her his own personal Lady Godiva. But that was the old Tyler, and obviously his tastes had changed.

"Keely?" Tyler stepped out of the bathroom and was patting aftershave on his cleanly shaven face. "Why aren't you in there visiting with Sheila?"

Keely shrugged her shoulders. "I don't know. I guess I don't feel like visiting with someone I don't know."

"Sheila's my right hand. You'll like her once you get to know her." Tyler pulled out a clean shirt from the top drawer of his dresser and began to unbutton the one he was wearing. Keely watched in misery as he pulled the old shirt off, revealing the broad expanse of his chest. She forced her eyes to focus on a picture hanging on the wall behind him. She felt her face grow slightly warm as he nonchalantly unzipped his trousers and stuffed the tail of his clean shirt into his pants.

"I won't be here long enough to get to know her," Keely reminded him, watching him rezip his trousers and buckle his belt. These were small things that she had seen him do hundreds of times in the past, but tonight they seemed to hold new fascination for her.

Picking up his hairbrush, Tyler ran it through the thick wiriness of his hair without replying to her statement. "Will you be all right here by yourself tonight?" he asked.

Keely yearningly watched the play of muscles across his back as he ran the brush through his hair one last time and laid it back down on the dresser. "I'll be fine."

Tyler turned, and for a moment his eyes were gentle and contemplative. "Are you sure?"

"I'm sure," she said softly. She was lying. She would never be fine again, and she knew it.

His large hand took her face and held it gently. The heartrending tenderness in his gaze forced her to fight even harder to stem the rising tears that threatened her eyes. "Where did we go wrong, Keely?"

Keely could only shake her head mutely, finding it impossible to answer his poignant query.

His finger reached out to lightly trace the outline of her mouth a moment before his lips slowly descended to meet hers. Two fat tears spilled over from her eyes as her lips parted slightly and she tilted her head up to him. He was going to kiss her, and there was nothing in the world she wanted more at this moment.

The soft knock on the bedroom door caused him to jerk away abruptly, his handsome face changing and becoming hard. "That's Sheila," he said curtly. "We have to go."

Keely brought her hand up to her mouth, the disappointment so acute it caused her stomach to contract painfully. She heard the bedroom door close, and once again she was without Tyler.

It was several minutes before she summoned the strength to leave the bedroom, where she felt a certain closeness to her estranged husband, a closeness she was reluctant to give up. Wiping away the last of her tears, she stiffened her back, straightened her blouse, blew her nose in a Kleenex, then went to join the dog in the kitchen. She knew she would be better off without Tyler. Now she had to make herself believe it.

As she entered the kitchen she saw the back of Poochie sticking out of the gigantic sack of dog food that sat in the utility room. She was going to have to move the sack where he couldn't keep getting into it. "Get out of that food, Poochie!" she scolded sharply. The dog's face came out of the sack with the speed of lightning, his large tail wagging happily. "And don't give me that innocent look," she threatened sternly as she walked over to start a load of clothes in the washer. Tyler needed some clean shirts, and she needed to wash the few things she had brought with her.

An hour later she was munching on an apple, deeply

engrossed in the TV show *Dallas* while she waited for the iron to heat. J.R. Ewing had just committed another dastardly deed, making her gasp with indignation as she picked up the iron and slapped it down thoughtlessly on one of Tyler's shirts. "Oh, shoot!" she exclaimed heatedly as she tried to lift the iron off the sticky fabric. She examined the ruined shirt in dismay. Well, she hoped it wasn't one of his favorites. She pitched it onto a kitchen chair, then turned back to what Miss Ellie was saying to Bobby. The next shirt turned out the same as the first and she balled it up and threw it on the floor. Ten minutes later Keely told Sue Ellen what she thought of her, then she glanced down and frowned in irritation. The scorched imprint of the iron decorated the middle of Tyler's gray dress shirt. *Damn! What kind of material do they make men's shirts out of lately,* she fumed silently as she slipped it on the hanger and headed for Tyler's bedroom. Hanging it in the back of the closet, she closed the door with a bang. That was the third shirt she had ruined this evening! She stomped back into the living room, having concluded that this had definitely not been her day. She picked up the two shirts and dumped them into the trash. She took the ironing board down and put it away. When she shopped for some clothes for herself tomorrow, she would buy him three new shirts and slip them into his drawer before he missed them.

"Poochie, get out of that dogfood," she shouted for the tenth time that evening. It was getting late, and she had hoped Tyler would be home by now so he could lift the heavy sack of food up on the utility room shelf. Obviously he was having too good a time to worry about his "wife" stuck home with a glutton that was consuming dogfood at the rate of roughly five pounds an hour! Determined to do the job herself, she hoisted the sack up on the washing machine, then paused to gather her strength. It was a fifty-pound sack, although she was reasonably sure the dog had eaten it down to thirty pounds. Giving a forceful heave, she got the sack balanced on her back and started to ease it toward the shelf over the washer. The sound of the sack's tearing caused her some momentary distress, but she figured she could get it up on the shelf before it tore enough to do any harm. Biting her lip, she eased the sack up a little farther, and the sound of tearing grew louder. Poochie stood watching her, his brown eyes riveted on the chunks of dogfood oozing out of the sack, down her neck. She bit her lip harder and looked around for help, afraid to move now for fear of being hit by an avalanche of dogfood. But what was she to do? It might be hours before Tyler could tear himself away from Sheila, and the sack was about to break her back. With a vigorous grunt, she heaved upward, just as the sack split wide open, sending a torrent of dogfood spraying across the room and on into the kitchen. Poochie took off like a bullet as he landed in the middle of the pile of dogfood and began to gobble up the unexpected feast. Keely slid down the length of the washing machine in dismay, her eyes disgustedly surveying the roomful of dry nuggets. She was literally buried in the foul-smelling mixture when Tyler came whistling in through the kitchen door.

He paused, his eyes glancing around the room blankly. "Hi, well, I see you're feeding the dog again." He continued to crunch his way over to the refrigerator and pull out a can of beer. Ripping the top off, he made a dramatic basket shot into the waste can, then took a long swig of the brew before he set it down on the counter.

Keely sat in the mound of dogfood, seething. If he wasn't enough of a gentleman to help her up, then he could just go hang!

"I don't know, Keely," he mused thoughtfully, "I don't think Sheila feeds him this much at one time. But then, what do I know about dogs!" He yawned, stretched, then picked up his can of beer and took one last fleeting look around. "Well, I'm going to hit the sack. I've got a long day tomorrow." He turned and crunched his way back out of the kitchen, never once looking back. He heard what to him sounded suspiciously like an enormous handful of dogfood hit the kitchen door as he shut it firmly behind him. His grin broadened and his step became jauntier as he chuckled his way back into his bedroom.

After spending another grueling eight hours on the living room couch, Keely was ready to throw in the towel. Her back felt as if it were broken in several different places, and her disposition was decidedly more cantankerous this morning than the previous one as she sat drinking her coffee. Something was going to have to be done. Soon!

Tyler came through the kitchen on his way to the laundry room, wearing only a pair of trousers, muttering under his breath about not being able to find any of his good shirts. Keely kept her eyes glued to the morning paper, hoping he would give up the search and settle for one of the older ones hanging in his closet.

Tyler stuck his head around the door of the utility room and addressed his wife. "Keely, have you seen my shirts?"

"Which one?" Her eyes didn't deviate a fraction from the Dear Abby column.

"The gray one."

"I think it's hanging in the back of your closet," she murmured, guilt written all over her face.

"Back of my closet!" he grumbled as he passed her in a dead run. "What in the hell is it doing there?"

Keely didn't really cherish the idea of telling him, so she buried her head deeper in the paper and, for once, kept quiet.

Ten minutes later Tyler strolled back into the kitchen, dressed in a charcoal gray suit . . . and the gray shirt. He poured himself a cup of coffee, dumped a slice of bread in the toaster, then took the chair opposite Keely.

"You wouldn't want to fill me in on why I'm going to work today in a shirt that has the scorched print of an iron on the back of it, would you?" he asked casually as he shook open the sports page of the paper and began to scan the headlines calmly.

Keely glanced up and grinned sheepishly. "Well, you see, Tyler, J. R. and Sue Ellen were in a terrible fight over the custody of the baby, and before I realized it, your shirt was scorched! But I'm going to buy you a new one when I go shopping this afternoon," she promised as he lowered the paper and arched his left eyebrow at her quizzically. She didn't dare tell him she had to buy him more than one shirt.

The paper was lowered another fraction of an inch as he studied her face intently, still trying to ascertain why he had the print of an iron on his shirt running up his back. Deciding that it would be more trouble to pursue the answer than it was worth, he shook his head wryly, then went back to the sports section. "I'll have to keep my jacket on all day. This one and my blue shirt are the only ones that match this suit, and I couldn't find the blue one."

"What would you like for supper tonight?" Keely asked brightly, trying to change the subject.

"The same thing I've had for the last two nights," he said dryly. "Nothing."

Keely looked up defensively. "*I* fixed dinner last night. Your choice, I might add."

"I'm going out for dinner tonight." He laid the paper down on the table and got up to retrieve his slice of toast. "We've been invited over to my partner's house."

"We?" Keely asked sullenly.

Tyler brought the toast back to the table and spread it thick with butter and strawberry jam.

"Yes, we. Chris and his wife would like to meet you. I accepted the invitation on our behalf."

"Well, thanks a lot, Tyler!" she said tightly. "What purpose could it serve for me to meet your business partner and his wife? After this week our 'marriage' will cease to exist. This inconsideration makes me downright ma . . ." Keely caught herself.

"Downright mad?" Tyler prompted in a sweet voice.

"No, er, downright glad, that I'll have the opportunity to show your friends that it wasn't *me* who was the culprit in this divorce," she said, improvising quickly.

"They're *my* friends, they know who the villain was," he reminded her with a sarcastic tinge in his voice.

"What have you told them!" she gasped, her temper surfacing.

"Tsk, tsk, tsk. Watch that tone of voice, sweetheart, it's edging on testy," he warned her as he finished off the slice of toast. "You better try to change the subject again, or you're going to be flying home tonight with only the clothes on your back as assets. I have an early appointment, so I need to be going," he said as he pushed away from the table and tweaked her nose in a gesture meant to irritate her. "Do we need anything from the store today? I'll pick it up on the way home."

Keely kept her gaze focused on her coffee cup, fighting the urge to let him have it with both barrels. There was no telling what he had told his friends about her! "I'd like some romance novels," she muttered absently, thinking she would enjoy reading while waiting for Tyler to come home.

Tyler was slipping his suit jacket on, barely listening to her. "I just bought the latest best seller the last time I went to the bookstore," he said, preoccupied with thoughts of his forthcoming meeting. "It's in the bedroom."

Keely lifted her head and met his eyes stonily, "I said *romance* novels, Tyler."

Tyler's face turned a shade paler now as her words penetrated. "You're kidding."

"No, I'm not kidding! I thought I would be back home by now, so I didn't bring any with me. Would you like me to write the names down on a piece of paper for you?" She hoped this would distress him to no end as she scribbled the titles of several books, more than she could ever read in a month.

"Please do, and pin it to my shirt for the whole world to see," he said irritably, taking a drink of his coffee. "Can't you buy them when you go shopping?"

"I'm not going in the direction of the bookstore. You're going right by it; can't you do this small favor for me?" she asked crossly.

"I'll do it, but you're really playing dirty now," he told her bluntly as she handed him the paper with twenty titles listed on it. He looked at it, then her, the anger slowly building in his eyes. "I have to buy all these books? You'll never read them all in the next few days."

"I'd like to have them in case I don't have time to look for them when I get home," she answered defiantly.

Now his anger was ready to explode, showering her with the steel sparks that glinted in his eyes. "How would *you* feel if I sent you down to the store to buy a dozen *Playboys*?"

"If you wanted them, I'd do it."

"I just bet you would! Let's drop the subject. I'll be home around six. Be ready," he said grumpily.

"Be ready!" she mimicked childishly behind his back as he stuffed a few loose papers into his briefcase. Brother, would she love to tell him where he could stick his dinner party, and his attitude!

"And, Keely, don't, I repeat, *don't* touch my den." He turned and fixed his steely-eyed gaze on her. "Do you understand?"

"You said I was to keep house and cook this week. I'm only doing my job," she reminded him coolly. "You *know* how I dislike clutter."

"I *know* how you'd dislike a broken neck more," he prodded at her pointedly. "Leave the den alone."

"Yes, King," she said in acknowledgment, springing to her feet to give him a dramatic curtsy. "I shall go about your kingdom with the utmost care today."

"See that you do," he said, ignoring her theatrical performance.

"Tyler, darling . . ." she said very sarcastically.

"Yes, sweetheart?" he replied more sarcastically.

"You won't be too surprised if you receive a call from me next week telling you what a jackass I think you are, will you, honey?" She grinned engagingly.

"Not at all, precious," he said, smiling back, "but due to your tight financial condition by that time, you'd better call after the rates change. I'm sure I'll have a few little things I'll want to say to you also." He reached over and gave her a peck on the cheek. "Gee, I'd forgotten how nice it is having a wife around in the mornings to get a man's day started off right. See you tonight . . . babykins."

Keely slammed her coffee cup down on the table as he exited the kitchen with a broad grin on his face. *I'm never going to make it four more days,* she thought in a panic. *I'll strangle him first!*

Within fifteen minutes she had the kitchen restored to order and decided to give some serious thought to what clothes she would need to purchase for the party and the remainder of her time here. She had hoped he would have lost his temper two days ago, and she would be back at her desk by now. He was deliberately holding his temper just to irritate her! Men! she seethed hotly.

As she passed through the living room her eyes fell on a gaily wrapped package sitting on the table where Tyler usually threw his keys. Approaching it cautiously, she tried to read the card without actually disturbing the package. After all, it was his apartment, and she shouldn't be snooping around, but still . . . By now she was practically standing on her head to read the name tag, to no avail. Glancing quickly at the door to be sure he wasn't going to reappear, she snatched the package up and read the words, "To Mitzi. One perfect woman."

Keely gripped the parcel tightly, wishing now she had left well enough alone. Not only did she have a Sheila to

69

contend with, but a "Mitzi, one perfect woman," had been thrown in. Her husband had been a busy man, she thought resentfully, reaching up to wipe angrily at a rebel tear. What possible difference could it make to her, she reasoned, swiping harder at the tears that seemed to be gathering with frightening momentum. Tyler was no longer answerable to her in any way, form, or fashion, so why should the knowledge that he was involved with at least two other women disturb her in the least! She didn't need him to exist, nor did she need him to make her life miserable with his petty bickering and unreasonable jealousy. Her life was her own, and she was going to be a gay, carefree, divorcee as soon as this whole ugly business was over and done with. That thought was most comforting, she considered bravely as she carefully placed the package back down on the table.

Turning away from the damning evidence that her marriage was indeed over, she walked over to the sofa and sank down on it tiredly. Since the tears seemed to persist in falling, she laid her head back on the cushion and stared up bleakly at a moth fluttering aimlessly around near the ceiling. If all these things were so reasonable, so comforting, then she couldn't help but wonder why, at that moment, she wished she were dead.

CHAPTER FIVE

"Well, I must say, Mrs. Jerico, you look beautiful tonight," Tyler complimented Keely as he helped her into his sporty red TR7. "I hope you remembered to buy me some shirts today?"

"I did," she assured him, reaching for her shoulder strap. She was glad he liked her new dress.

"Good," he said as he got in on his side and buckled his seat belt. "There were at least two occasions today when I thought I was going to expire from a heat stroke."

"I was able to find one the same shade as your old one," Keely said proudly, "even though it did take three hours of hard shopping."

Tyler glanced at her and grinned. "Thanks, I appreciate your effort."

"You're welcome," she said, smiling back pleasantly.

"You know, I was thinking this afternoon, Keely, it isn't so hard to control our tempers when we put our minds to it," he said as he merged the small car into the traffic.

Keely smothered a chuckle. *Maybe it hadn't been hard for him!*

"I wonder why we didn't try harder to get along

71

before," he mused softly. He seemed to have forgotten her presence for the moment. "Thinking back over our marriage, the things we fought most often about were not major problems, nothing we couldn't have sat down and talked about sensibly."

"I know," she said tiredly as she watched the passing traffic. He wasn't saying anything that she hadn't said to herself a million times since they separated. "I suppose that there are just some people who can't get along with each other."

"Yes, I suppose that's true," Tyler said quietly. They drove for a minute more in silence, then he added in a gentle tone, "It wasn't because I didn't love you, Keely, you know that, don't you?"

"You said you loved me," she whispered painfully.

"It was just that you could make me so damn mad . . . and jealous. . . ." His voice cracked.

"I never looked at another man, Tyler," she defended herself wearily. "I know what you think about Craig Easton, but you're wrong. I had every opportunity to marry Craig before I met you, but I didn't. I married you."

"I've had a lot of lonely nights to think about our situation, Keely, and I'll admit I was unreasonable at times, but the thought of you in any other man's arms could send me out of my mind. If there was nothing between you and Craig, why didn't you tell him to get lost!"

"He represented a large account for my father's construction firm, Tyler, you knew that! What was I supposed to do, kick him out the front door every time he walked in and said good morning to me? He never made any kind of a pass at me, or I would have done just that. If you had really loved me, you would have trusted me."

"If you had loved *me*, you would have told that guy to go to hell," Tyler responded in a strained voice. "You knew how he upset me."

"Everything upset you!" Keely said tightly.

"The hell it did! You were the one who always got all bent out of shape when I tried to discuss Craig with you." Tyler said the words calmly, but his twitching jaw told another story. "*I* was not the one who was unreasonable. You know full well you had me wrapped around your little finger. Rarely was I the instigator of our disagreements."

"Ha! If that isn't a big laugh. *I* was the one that went out of my way to avoid squabbles with you. I was *not* the one who was hard to get along with."

"Yes, you were," he said calmly. He signaled to switch driving lanes. From the corner of her eye Keely caught a glimpse of a fast-approaching car trying to merge from an outer ramp. Her hand clamped down on Tyler's leg like a vise.

"That car's trying to butt in line! Slow down!" she shouted.

"Damn! Get your fingernails out of my thigh." He took her hand and pried it off of his trousers. "I saw the car!" He fought to regain control of the wheel.

"You don't have to be rude!" she said hostilely, jerking her hand out of his. "I merely pointed out the car was coming at us too fast. See! That's exactly what I've been talking about; *you* get so darned upset over every teeny thing."

"Teeny thing! Do you have any idea how that drives me up the wall when you sit over there and stomp the floorboard, grip the dash, and scream at me over all the imagined cars that are going to wipe us out! Hell, a man could have a nervous breakdown just driving down the block with you!" he raved hotly.

The little red sports car shot off the exit ramp, its two occupants glaring stonily ahead into the night.

"You always did drive too fast."

"Will you just let me do the driving and content yourself with bitching quietly to yourself!" he said with firm finality. "I haven't killed us yet."

By the time they reached the Morgans, there was no longer any danger of either one of them losing the bet. They were permanently not speaking to each other. Tyler broke the cold silence as he helped her out of the car.

"Try to control yourself while we're here. The Morgans are good friends of mine." He handed her the package addressed to Mitzi. "Here, carry this."

Keely's eyebrows flew up in disbelief. "You want me to carry your . . . your girl friend's package," she managed to spit out indignantly.

"My what?"

"Your girl friend! The one besides Sheila!" she enunciated clearly.

"Sheila! Good Lord, I think someone's blown out your pilot light, Keely. Where in the hell did you get the idea Sheila was anything but a secretary to me?"

"Isn't she?" she sneered.

"That happens to be none of your damn business!" he said, slamming the car door with an authoritative bang.

"Then you carry your own stinkin' package," she said, thrusting the box out and hitting his chest with a thud. "And just because my voice sounds angry, don't get any funny ideas, mister. It just *sounds* mad. I'm not!" With one last withering perusal of the package, she whirled and started up the walk.

"Are you sure you're not mad?" he called sweetly after her.

"Hell, *no,* I'm not mad! Now, are you coming or not? These aren't my friends, you know!"

By the time the door was answered, Tyler and Keely had managed to paste smiles on their faces, ready to greet their host and hostess for the evening.

Sheila opened the door. *Well, hell's bells! I suppose he's going to have his entire harem here to torment me tonight,* Keely thought rebelliously as she walked rudely past her on into the house, saying curtly, "What's for dinner? I haven't had a decent meal in days."

"Tyler, Keel . . ." Sheila glanced at Tyler questioningly. Tyler shrugged his broad shoulders and grinned apologetically. "Hi!"

Sheila smiled back knowingly and held the door open wider for him to pass through. "Good evening, Tyler."

Keely had marched her way into the living room, disregarding the fact that she had never been in the house before, and sat down on the couch. If he thought she was going to "control" herself under these circumstances, then *he* was the one playing with a warped hockey stick!

"You'll have to excuse my wife," Tyler was saying to Sheila, "she's had a bad day."

"She's had a bad year," Keely said snidely. "Can I have a glass of wine?"

"Certainly," Sheila acquiesced, walking over to the small bar. "How about you, Tyler?"

"Scotch and water."

The corner of Sheila's mouth twitched as she tried to overcome the impulse to burst out laughing. By the looks on the Jericos' faces, all was not well.

"Tyler!" The kitchen door opened, and a cute blonde walked into the room. A sandy-haired man followed in her path, munching on a piece of celery stuffed with cheese. Tyler stood up, taking the hand that was extended to him in a friendly greeting.

"Pam, good to see you again."

"Aren't you glad to see me again?" Chris asked as he licked the remaining cheese off his fingers. "It's been at least two hours since we last saw each other."

"Has it been two hours?" Tyler asked in surprise. "My, how time flies when your havin' fun."

"Okay, buddy, one of these days you're going to realize who's the real brains of the business and start showing me more respect," Chris said, grinning and slapping his partner in a jovial show of affection. "Where's Keely?"

"Sulking over on the couch."

Keely stiffened resentfully as Sheila handed her the glass of white wine.

"Tyler!" Pam said chidingly as she walked over and extended a hand to Keely. "Hello, Keely, I'm Pam Morgan."

"I'm pleased to meet you." Keely was touched by the almost imperceptible squeeze of assurance Pam gave her hand. "And I think you've met Sheila."

"Yes, we have met."

"Mitzi isn't here yet. She called and said she was going to be late," Pam said, then sat down next to Keely and motioned with her hand for the other three to take a seat. "The extra time will give us the opportunity to get acquainted with Keely."

"So, this is your . . . wife." Chris was smiling as he took a chair next to Tyler.

"Yes, I'm the devious witch he married," Keely said, draining her glass of wine in one long swallow. Extending her empty glass to Sheila, she smiled sweetly and said, "Hit me again."

Sheila's mouth dropped open slightly before she recovered gracefully and accepted the glass. "Does your drink need freshening, Tyler?" she asked with a giggle.

Tyler glanced down at the glass in his hand, which Sheila had handed him a minute earlier. "No, I'm nursing this one along," he said dryly.

Chris laughed openly. "Having a little problem, Ty?"

Tyler wasn't smiling now as he took a drink of the Scotch, then set the glass on the coffee table. "I'm sorry, Keely and I are not in the best of moods tonight. I hope you'll overlook *her* bad manners." He glared accusingly over in the direction of the sofa.

Pam shook her head worriedly and reached for Keely's hand once more. "I know this is going to sound strange to you, Keely, but I feel that I know you, even though we've just met. Tyler has told us so much about you."

"I can imagine." Keely took another drink of her wine.

She was uncomfortable with the easy familiarity the Morgans were showing her. She didn't want to like *his* friends, and she was equally sure they wouldn't care much for her.

"No, it isn't what you think," she said gently, her eyes meeting Keely's, those of one who understood how she felt.

Keely's gaze lowered to her glass. "Tyler's right. I hope you forgive my rudeness. I shouldn't have come tonight," she said softly and repentantly.

"Nonsense." Pam dismissed what she'd said. "We are very happy to have you as our guest. Sheila, Chris, and I are well aware of the divorce that's pending between you and Ty, but that doesn't mean we can't all enjoy an evening together." She looked over and smiled at Tyler encouragingly. "It happens in the best of families."

Chris got up from his chair and walked over to the bar to pour himself a drink. "It's really none of my business, but did you two ever think of sitting down and *discussing* your problems instead of trying to slug them out verbally?"

"*I've* tried," Tyler said curtly.

Keely snorted softly in exasperation, then drained her glass again.

"If you'll excuse me, I think I'll check on the dinner," Sheila said, discreetly getting up to leave the room.

Naturally, Keely thought resentfully, Sheila wouldn't want to see her lover's dirty laundry being aired so openly. *Keely* didn't even want to see it aired so openly!

"Fix me a Perrier with a twist of lime, will you, darling?" Pam called to her husband as she kicked off her shoes and stretched her legs out on the coffee table before her. "You don't mind if I get comfortable, do you?" She glanced at Keely sheepishly.

Keely smiled, the first since she arrived. "No, not at all."

"As I was saying," Chris said, handing his wife her drink, "all married couples have quarrels. I've always told

77

Pammy that fighting is just as important as loving. In a good marriage there's a necessity for both."

Pam's laugh broke the tension that had hovered in the air as she accepted the drink and a short kiss from her husband. "If Chris and I had thought of divorce every time we disagreed about something, we would have been married roughly one week! Do you know what our first real fight was over? The way Chris kept jerking too hard on the shower curtain, pulling it out of the hooks and never bothering to put it back. Every time I'd go into that bathroom and see that shower curtain sagging, I'd see red!"

Chris joined her laughter, taking a seat next to Tyler. "That was only the first of many. The second day of our honeymoon we got in a fight over where we were going to eat."

"That was entirely your fault, Christopher!"

"Now, how do you figure that?" He turned to face Tyler. "Here we are, on our honeymoon, and the last thing on my mind was food, but my wife says she's starving to death! We go out, get in the car we rented, and start driving. 'What do you want to eat?' I asked. 'I don't know. Let's see if we can find something that looks really appealing,' she said. Two hours later we were still looking for something that looked appealing to her! By now I was starving to death and growing meaner by the minute."

"I'll drink to that," Pam said, raising her glass toward her husband.

Keely giggled. "Did you ever eat?"

"Yes, we finally stopped at an all-night hamburger joint and had a bowl of chili. I lived on Rolaids for the next two days," Chris said, grinning.

"That reminds me of the first fight Keely and I had," Tyler joined in. "I didn't have the faintest idea I was marrying such a perfectionist. She's a compulsive cleaner! Before I got up the nerve to lay the law down to her, she used to wake me up on Saturday mornings running the

78

vacuum cleaner at seven in the morning. And on Sundays I'd jump out of bed, looking forward to a quiet morning of having a leisurely cup of coffee and reading my fishing magazines. I'd sort out the magazines I wanted to study closer and lay them next to my chair in the living room, then go to the kitchen for my coffee. By the time I'd get back, she would have already thrown the magazines back in the rack and vacuumed around my chair again. I'd be ready to break her arm!"

"Tyler, you have no idea how frustrating it is to get the apartment all cleaned up then come back to a bunch of magazines scattered all over the floor!" Keely protested. "And I wasn't the only one who did irritating things." She turned to plead her case to Pam. "He had the nerve-racking habit of leaving the toilet seat up! I'd get up in the middle of the night too sleepy to turn a light on and nearly drown myself when I fell into the toilet!"

"I told you I was sorry about that!" Tyler said seriously. "It was just a bad habit I had from being a bachelor for so long."

"I was getting used to it," Keely murmured, trying to avoid his gaze. "I should have turned on the light and watched what I was doing."

"And the fight we had about the grocery shopping," Tyler continued. "I know that got completely out of hand, and I shouldn't have been so steamed about it, but every time you brought it up it made me mad all over again." He finally captured her eyes. "I've always wanted to tell you I'm sorry about that."

"What happened?" Pam asked, enjoying the conversation.

"When I would send Tyler shopping for groceries, he would come back with four sacks of groceries—and nothing to eat. The argument he's referring to happened one day when I sent him to the store for milk and he came back with sixteen cans of bug spray! 'It was on sale,' he'd announced proudly. Every time I opened the cabinet and saw those cans of bug spray, I wanted to scream!"

"Yes, and every time I walked into the kitchen after that and asked, 'What's for supper?' she'd smart off and say, 'Bug spray.' "

The four occupants of the room burst out laughing. "You think that's bad!" Pam said, dying to get out her "topper." "One time Chris bought an industrial-size jar of olives for the two of us! We ate olives every day for one solid year!"

"But does Chris ever go in and open a can of frozen grapefruit juice, fix one glass, then leave the rest to spoil?" Keely asked as she glanced at Tyler and smiled shyly.

"Does Pam ever dump her flowery bubble bath in the tub while your back's turned because she doesn't want a ring left in the tub?" Tyler grinned at her, his eyes glowing with a loving warmth. "I couldn't believe one woman could move so fast. I would only be gone a second."

"You always smelled nice afterward!" she laughed, returning his gaze with affection.

"Do you know, Chris, that we actually wasted one whole day arguing over whether the color of our bedroom was blue or green?"

The smiles began to fade slowly from Tyler's and Keely's faces as they described aloud some of the petty, immaterial things that had gotten in the way of their love for each other. Hearing them spoken out loud was a sobering experience for them both.

Pam leaned her head back on the cushioned softness of the sofa and closed her eyes. "I once knew a couple that swore that after twenty years of marriage, they had never fought. But the anger between them was so tangible that you could see the hostility in the way they passed each other in a room!"

"I used to worry about the children that Pam and I want some day," Chris admitted. "Pam and I can get in some humdingers of fights at times. But I think that it's

80

healthy for parents to argue in front of kids. It shows the kids that the parents are being open and honest about how they feel." He paused, then went on. "But fighting all the time makes kids feel threatened and insecure, and that's the last thing Pam and I would want."

Pam smiled at her husband, her face leaving no doubt that the Morgans had a very healthy marriage. "Chris and I have always felt that real communication can begin when two people let down their defenses and tell the other one what's really buggin' them. A man, for instance, is sometimes unable to admit when he's feeling hurt or needs some extra attention, so he may channel these emotions into a quarrelsome behavior, and pick a fight."

Keely glanced up at Tyler, a bell ringing in the back of her subconscious mind. Was that one of the problems that had caused her husband to be so moody and insecure at times? She knew his life had not been as secure as most children's, having grown up in those foster homes. Had she failed to extend to him an extra amount of attention, an extra dose of affection, something a person sometimes needed so desperately in his life? She had never stopped to think about it. She had been raised in a home with an overabundance of love; she had never needed assurance about being loved. Even though Tyler was a very stable person, a childhood such as his would have had to have caused scars.

"It all comes down to the simple fact—you either love a person enough to wade through all the problems, or you don't," Chris concluded. "Life isn't perfect; neither are people. It's much too easy nowadays, if things don't go the way a person dreamed they would, to walk away from the marriage and look for that cloud with the silver lining. As a rule, it's never found, and a person ends up with more problems than he originally started out with."

"Chris, are you saying that the grass doesn't look green-er on the other side to you?" Pam teased.

"My dear wife," Chris said lovingly, "you are as green as I can handle!"

Pam's face turned blank. "Thank you—I think!"

Keely cast another peek from beneath her long lashes toward Tyler. Though he was not looking at her, his face spoke for him. Chris and Pam had given him food for thought.

"There's Mitzi!" Pam announced reluctantly reaching for her shoes. "I'll get the door."

"I'll go with you," Chris offered, taking his wife's hand and pulling her up off the couch. "Fix yourself another drink, Ty, Keely. It will still be a few minutes before we eat."

The Morgans left the room, and an uneasy silence descended over the couple left alone. Tyler walked over to the bar and stood for a moment, staring down at the assorted decanters of liquors before him. Dipping his head slightly, he said in a strained voice, "Damn it, Keely, why couldn't we have had a marriage like theirs?"

"Apparently they worked at their happiness; we didn't." That fact seemed glaringly clear at the moment. Unfortunately it was too late to correct or retract all the unkind words, the hurtful accusations, that they had said to each other in the heat of anger. Keely had read numerous articles on troubled marriages and knew that once the pattern of bickering was firmly established in a relationship, moving beyond petty squabbling was rarely easy. She knew a marriage counselor would help them to explore their problems, but they had gotten into a fight over which doctor they would consult when they had tried to discuss that alternative. Their marriage was hopeless.

Tyler spread his hands out before him on the smooth surface of the padded bar and shrugged his shoulders. "Maybe we should think about trying again," he said quietly.

Keely's pulse leapt at his words, fighting the urge to throw caution to the wind and fall into his arms, agreeing to anything as long as it meant they would be together once more. But nothing had changed. They were the same two people who were unable to stay in the same room together without finding fault with the other one.

"I don't think so," she whispered almost inaudibily.

He turned and stared at her for many long moments. "Do you know that I would give everything I owned right now to kiss you," he said huskily.

Keely's eyes flew up to meet his, astounded at his unexpected words. She didn't know how to answer him. Should she tell him she would pay that price, and more, if he would take her in his arms and, for just a few brief minutes, let her feel his mouth hungrily exploring hers? Her gaze fell back to her hands, which lay lifelessly in her lap. She was unwilling to face him, yet unwilling to give up the slender thread of intimacy that seemed to have sprung up unexpectedly between the two of them. "I can't see where that would help matters any."

It took but a second for him to cover the distance between them. Gently he eased down before her and repeated softly, "I *want* to kiss my wife. I've wanted to since the day you first got here, and I'm tired of playing games with you."

Keely reached out and touched his familiar face gently with trembling fingers. "If you ever once touched me, Tyler, I'd be lost. Can't you see that things will not work out for us? It's best if we keep this divorce as smooth and uncomplicated as possible."

"No, I'm finding that very hard to believe right now," he said sincerely. "All I can see is the blue of your eyes, the way they sparkle when you laugh, the way your mouth begs to be kissed, the way your hair covers your shoulders like soft velvet—those are the only things I can see clearly right now, Keely."

"My hair is too long . . . too unfashionable . . ." Keely murmured inanely, drowning in his gray eyes, which glowed with a savage inner fire.

83

"Your hair's beautiful, and don't change the subject," he whispered with a deep timbre in his voice. "Are you going to let me kiss you or not?"

"Uh . . . mmm . . . excuse me," Pam said quietly and apologetically from the entrance to the living room. "Mitzi's here, and dinner is served."

Tyler's gaze never left his wife's. "Thanks, Pam, we'll be right there."

He reached for Keely's hand and helped her up from the couch. Her knees felt too weak now to support her slight frame.

"Hey, you two," Chris greeted them, walking through the door with a lovely white-haired lady holding his arm, "the guest of honor's arrived!"

"Mitzi!" Tyler walked over and affectionately kissed her on her forehead. "How's my favorite birthday girl?"

"Another year older, and deeper in debt," Mitzi laughed, patting him affectionately on the back. "How's my favorite man?"

"Fine, and you look beautiful." He held her away from him to survey her plumpish figure. "You've got curves in all the right places."

"And all the wrong ones too," Mitzi said with a frown. "Don't try to use your flattery on an old woman, Tyler Jerico."

"Mitzi, I've told you a million times, I'm older than you are. I just happen to be an extremely youthful-looking eighty-year-old man."

She took a playful swat at him. "What am I going to do with you!"

"Not much. You just have to take me as I am," he said seriously.

Mitzi had a stern look on her face as she peeked around Tyler's broad shoulders to confront Keely. "Does this belong to you?"

No, Keely thought sadly. *Not anymore.*

84

"Mom, this is Keely," Chris introduced them, taking Keely's hand. "Keely, this lovely lady is my mother."

Keely felt a slow blush color her face as she met Tyler's knowing eyes. Mitzi, one perfect woman was Chris Morgan's mother.

"Hello, Mitzi," Keely said, taking her hand. "Is this your birthday?"

"I'm afraid so," she sighed.

"Now, Mom, you're not getting older, you're just getting better," Chris assured her as he took her arm and steered her toward the kitchen. "And if we don't hurry and eat the supper Pam's slaved over all evening, none of us are going to live to see your next one!"

The next few hours were spent in a party atmosphere. Keely found herself laughing at the teasing antics the two men directed toward Mitzi. Several times during the course of the evening she felt Tyler's eyes on her, and a warm glow overtook her. She would caution herself that no matter what mood he was in tonight there was still a very important bet between them. If he were trying to lull her into a state of laxity, then he would be in for a surprise.

It would be just like him to make her think he was mellowing out, then pull something unexpected that would send her into a frenzy! He was ruthless when it came to winning a bet, and she was going to have to be alert for any of his devious tricks! She had to bear in mind she wouldn't have money for even bus fare home if she lost.

Keely kept a wary eye on Tyler and Sheila at the dinner table. They were so comfortable with each other that Keely felt the pangs of jealousy several times, and with Sheila being Chris's sister no wonder Tyler was treated like a member of the family. Even though they had been exceptionally nice to her, Keely felt that they were only biding time until Tyler was free of his past and could marry into their happy midst.

Keely couldn't seem to keep her eyes off Sheila's hair. It looked so saucy, so perky! Her hand kept wandering up to her long mane, and she toyed with it, wrapping it around her finger absently. What would she look like in a style like that? Would Tyler look at her the way he was looking at Sheila right now? A gleam of admiration on his face? Maybe that had been part of their problem. Perhaps she should have been more stylish. Men wanted to feel proud of their wives, didn't they? Tyler would probably have appreciated the fact that she had followed the trend of fashion, even though he had insisted he liked her hair the way it was.

As they were saying good night, Keely found the opportunity to speak with Sheila alone. "I love your hair," she said sincerely. "Would you mind giving me the name of your beautician?"

"Of course not, but surely you're not thinking of doing anything different with your gorgeous hair, are you?" she asked in surprise.

"Oh, I don't know," Keely hedged, "I've been thinking of doing something for a change, and since I'm not working this week, I thought this might be a good time."

"Gosh," Sheila said, admiring Keely's thick, lustrous hair, "if I had hair like that, I'd never dream of changing it!"

"A shorter style would be easier to take care of," Keely protested meekly.

"Well," Sheila said, picking up a pad and writing down a name and telephone number, "just tell Judy that I sent you; she'll work you in some way." Casting one last admiring glance at Keely's hair, she said, "Isn't that funny. You have something I've always wanted, and you're wanting to get rid of it! No wonder men think women are crazy," she laughed.

Keely laughed with her, but her mind was elsewhere. She knew that Sheila was referring to her hair when she said Keely had something she wanted. But, ironically, the thought surfaced in Keely's mind that Sheila, too, had something that she had always wanted: Tyler.

The ride back to the apartment was made in silence. Tyler had seemed to forget his intentions of kissing his wife. He barely looked at her and said very little.

As they let themselves into the apartment, Keely's eyes focused on the sofa that was to be her bed for several more nights, and her back protested with a painful spasm. "Tyler, why don't we change beds for the next couple of days?" Keely suggested impetuously.

Tyler whirled and looked at her. "No way! I told you, I'm not sleeping on that sofa."

"Don't you think that's being just a tiny bit unfair?" she said, reasoning patiently. "I've slept on that sofa for the last two nights, and my back's killing me. We can take turns as long as I'm here, then neither one of us will have to suffer for any long period of time."

"I don't plan on suffering for even a short period of time," he announced firmly. "I am *not* sleeping on that sofa."

Keely's temper flared. "Well, I'm not either," she said coldly. "If you're going to be a hog and take the only decent bed in the house, then I'm sleeping in it with you."

"Say what?" he asked, grinning.

"I'm sleeping in your bed tonight. If you don't like it, you can lump it!"

Tyler had a definite smirk on his face. "I didn't say I wouldn't like it."

"You can wipe that stupid grin off your face this instant, Tyler. I'll be *sleeping* in your bed, nothing else."

"You have a dirty mind, did you know that, Mrs. Jerico? What ever gave you the idea that I thought you'd be doing anything else?"

Keely swept by him regally. "It isn't *my* mind that's dirty . . . Mr. Jerico."

Fifteen minutes later she came out of the small bathroom, feeling a little self-conscious in her short nightgown, but scolding herself for feeling like a silly teenager. After all, they were married, and he had seen her hundreds of times in her nightgown, and less.

Tyler was sitting on his side of the bed, setting the alarm clock as she finished rubbing hand lotion on her hands, then crawled in bed on her side. He switched off the light, and she heard his robe hit the floor. Her eyes widened in the dark as she belatedly recalled how he had always slept in the nude.

"I hope you're decent," she said tightly as she scooted as far over on her side as the bed allowed.

"Have you ever known me to be decent," he said, bored, as he fluffed up his pillow and sank down into it.

"I meant, I hope you have . . . pajamas on," she clarified.

"Pajamas!" he said indignantly. You would have thought she had accused him of wearing a ruffled negligee!

"Pajamas or . . . something!"

"You're perfectly aware of my sleeping habits. If you don't like them, go back to the couch," he snapped rudely.

Keely turned over and punched her pillow with a vicious whack!

"Ouch," Tyler said tauntingly.

Keely refused to answer him. She snuggled down more comfortably into the softness of the bed. It felt absolutely heavenly after the past two nights on the concrete slab. At least Poochie wouldn't be waking her up at the crack of dawn anymore. Sheila had taken him back to her apartment today. This bed was the most comfortable bed she had ever slept in, she mused, squirming deeper into its warmth. It seemed to float and move when she turned. All of a sudden Keely sat bolt upright, her blue eyes blazing fire. "Good grief, Tyler! This is a waterbed!"

Tyler had been just about to doze off when she had shouted out at him. "What!" He sat up in a daze.

She turned in the dark, and faced him ominously, "I said, this is a waterbed!"

"Well, hell, Keely! I'm glad you told me," he mumbled irritably, jerking the covers back over himself angrily. "I would have never guessed."

Keely sat there in the middle of the waterbed, feeling absolutely miserable. What was her husband doing with a . . . a . . . waterbed! It seemed almost indecent to her. She glanced up suspiciously at the ceiling.

"What are you looking for now, mirrors?" Tyler asked sleepily.

Darn him, he must have the eyes of a cat! Keely sat staring in the dark, her mind conjuring up a multitude of sins that surely had taken place in this room. How many times had Sheila been here in this very bed! Tyler grumbled a low expletive and sat up in bed.

"All right. What's wrong with me having a waterbed? You know we talked about buying one several times," he reminded her gently.

"Yes, I know *we* did. But this is different!"

Tyler sighed and laid his head back against the headboard. "Why is it different?"

"Well . . . you know . . ." Keely felt embarrassed.

"Because everyone says they're great to make love in, right?"

"Yes!" Her feelings were very hurt. Tyler had gone too far this time.

"They also happen to be very therapeutic for a bad back."

Keely faced him accusingly in the dark. "You don't have a bad back," she pointed out.

"At my age, I could develop one at any time," he reasoned defensively.

Keely glared at him, hating the overwhelming feeling of jealousy that assaulted her. With one last contemptuous flick of her eyes, she lay back down and rolled back to her edge of the bed.

Tyler stayed in his position, staring up at the dark ceiling.

He was going to be very lucky if she ever spoke to him again! And if he thought for one minute that she would lower herself to ask him what it was like to actually make love in a waterbed, well, he was just plain off his rocker. She had some pride.

"What's it like to make love in a waterbed?" Darn! She could bite her tongue off.

"I wouldn't know," Tyler said, the grin in his voice coming through.

Keely had been holding herself so tense that her body ached. At his encouraging words she felt some of the tension drain from her.

"You're not lying to me, Tyler, are you?" she whispered hopefully.

"No, I'm not lying to you, Keely." She could tell by the tone of his voice he was telling her the truth.

"Well, just so you don't get the wrong idea," she said sheepishly in a small voice, "I just want you to know I'm only making idle conversation."

"Of course. Can we go to sleep now?"

"Yes." Keely had to fight to keep the happiness from bubbling out in her voice. She knew he had only admitted to not making love in this waterbed, and she knew that there were other places for people to make love, but it made her feel a whole lot better knowing nothing had happened in this immediate vicinity.

"Good night, Mrs. Jerico."

"Good night, Mr. Jerico."

She smiled into the darkness and snuggled down closer to her husband. Yes, a waterbed was definitely therapeutic.

CHAPTER SIX

The sound of running water and a man whistling woke Keely early the next morning. She lay quietly, savoring the sound of Tyler taking his shower. She had heard that sound so many times before and had always taken it for granted. Now it was something she wanted to tuck away in a secret place to take back home with her. Rolling over on his side of the bed, she grabbed his pillow and hugged it tightly. "Good morning, my sweet, sexy husband," she said, kissing it with exuberance. She smothered the pillow in kisses again, smacking loudly, and giggling wickedly.

"You got a thing for pillows now, Keely?"

Keely dropped the pillow and lay very still.

"Well?"

"Well, what?" she asked calmly, wishing the roof would fall in right about now.

"Are you going to tell me why you were molesting my pillow?" He grinned, rubbing his hair dry with a towel.

"Molesting your pillow! I was merely fluffing it up so I wouldn't have to when I made the bed. Honestly, Tyler," she scolded, "your mind's always in the gutter." She summoned the nerve to roll over and face him, then immediately wished she hadn't. He was standing next to the bed with only a towel draped around his midsection, looking ten times more handsome than any man had a right to look. Her heart hammered against her ribs as he walked over to the closet and removed a pair of dark trousers.

"Sleep any better last night?"

"Considerably. I'm a bit seasick this morning," she grinned impishly, "but definitely more rested."

"Just think how rested you would have been if we had tried out that waterbed theory," he said nonchalantly as he selected an appropriate tie.

Keely sat up in bed, suddenly anxious to escape from his disturbing presence. "Do you want me to fix your breakfast?"

"No," he said. There was just the faintest glint of humor in his eyes. "I only have time for one the other—I choose the waterbed."

"Tyler." Keely didn't care if he was her husband; he was embarrassing her. "Don't talk that way!"

Tyler cocked one eyebrow quizzically. "Why not?"

"Because," she said as she lay back down, "have you forgotten we're in the process of a divorce?"

He gave an ironic chuckle as he reached into his drawer for a clean shirt. "Hardly. But what's that got to do with me wanting to try out the waterbed?"

"I don't believe you're for real," she said crossly. "I suppose you want to . . . try out the waterbed, then sign the divorce papers."

"No," he paused in his dressing, a thoughtful look creasing his brow. "I want to win the bet, try out the waterbed, *then* I'll think about signing the divorce papers."

Keely picked up her pillow and threw it at him. "You're *not* winning the bet, and you *are* signing the papers. That was the agreement."

He held up his trousers, grinning broadly. "Do you want to lie there and drool over what you're missing, or do you want to turn your head while I put my underwear and trousers on?"

"What would you do if I said I wanted to watch," Keely said smugly, taunting him now.

"I'd sing three verses of 'Red Hot Mama!' "

Keely rolled back over to face the other side of the wall. "Tyler, you did agree to sign those papers, you know," she reminded him seriously. "I've been here four days now, and I'll be going home in another three. Ty, I've been thinking, what happens if neither one of us wins the bet?"

"I don't know," Tyler conceded quietly.

"Well, I hope I win," she admitted. "I'm going to be in a bind if I don't."

"Aren't you getting married after the divorce? You can turn back around now." Tyler slid his belt through the loops of his pants, watching her face for a reaction.

"Who, me? No, I don't think I'll ever get married again." Her fingers plucked at the blanket, "What about you?"

"I don't plan on it anywhere in the near future."

"Sheila isn't pressing you to get married?"

Tyler finished tying his shoe and stood up. "No harder than Craig's pressing you apparently."

Keely sighed. "I'm not going to marry Craig. You know that; why do you insist on beating a dead horse?"

Tyler laid his hairbrush back down on the dresser carefully. She could see his eyes searching her face intently in the mirror in front of him. "I'm going to ask you this one more time, Keely, then I'll make you a promise that I'll never bring it up again. In view of the fact we're getting a divorce anyway, I want the truth. Has there ever been anything between you and Craig since we married?"

There was an almost lethal calmness in her eyes now as she stared back at his reflection in the mirror. "There has never been anything between Craig Easton and me. Neither before, or after, I married you," she said in a steady voice.

It seemed a very long time before either of them could make themselves turn away from the other's gaze. Keely knew that she didn't have to answer his question. What did it matter now? But for some inexplicable reason, she wanted him to know the truth.

"Then I owe you an apology," Tyler said softly.

"You owe me nothing," Keely said. "If you believe me, that's all I want."

"All right," he said, his voice trembling with emotion. "I do believe you."

Keely closed her eyes, breathing a prayer of thanks. It seemed as if a heavy stone had rolled away from her heart. "Thank you."

Tyler walked slowly over to the bed and knelt down beside her. Keely felt the rush of tears spring to her eyes as he gazed at her compassionately and magnetically. The smell of his aftershave, the feel of his hand as he picked up one of hers and brought it to his lips, both served to make her tears flow harder and faster. "What have I done to us, Keely?" he murmured huskily as he tenderly kissed each fingertip. "Oh, God, what have I done?"

"Ty," she sobbed, her heart nearly breaking at his desolation. "Ty . . . don't."

He reached out and caught her lovely head in his hands, pulling her close to him. She buried her face in the warmness of his neck, letting the tears have their own way now. His tears began to mingle with hers as they cried away months of bitterness, months of regret, together. But there had been too much hurt to put aside, too many misunderstandings in their rocky marriage, to cleanse their feelings completely. Tyler held her in his arms a few minutes more before he released her and slowly rose to his feet. He stroked her hair lovingly for a moment; then, without a word, he picked up his jacket and walked quietly out of the bedroom. There was nothing left to say. "Sorry" was no longer enough.

The day dragged by for Keely. All she wanted was to

go home now and try to forget her disastrous marriage. It no longer mattered to her if she won the bet or not. Either way, she was going to be left with nothing.

Around noon she had finished her housework and was sitting down to a light lunch when she caught her reflection in the small mirror over the kitchen sink. Sheila's image flashed into her mind again. Sheila with the bouncy, sexy hair. Sheila, who had Tyler now. Laying down her sandwich, she walked over and picked up her purse. Searching through the contents for a moment, she finally produced a piece of paper with the name of Sheila's beauty operator written on it. Before she changed her mind, she picked up the phone and dialed the number. When she hung up, she had an appointment for two o'clock.

The phone rang again as she was getting ready to leave the apartment. Debating whether to let it ring or answer it, curiosity got the best of her, and she snatched it up on the fifth ring. "Hello!"

"Keely?" It was Tyler. "Where were you? I was just about to hang up."

"I was getting ready to go out."

"Where were you going?" he asked.

"Oh, just out." She wanted to surprise him with the fashionable "new Keely."

"Oh." Tyler's voice sounded disappointed. "Are you going to be gone long? I thought I might knock off early and take you for a ride in the mountains."

"Oh, that would be nice, Tyler, but I don't think I can today." Keely bit her lip, hoping he wouldn't press her on her plans.

"What could you possibly have to do in a town you're unfamiliar with?" he asked petulantly.

"Oh, I thought I might go over to a K mart and look around. Where is one?" she asked quickly.

"A K mart? Hell, I don't know. I think there's one over on Circle and Airport Road." There was a moment of silence. "You'd rather go browse around in a K mart than go for a drive with me?" His voice sounded hurt and a little incredulous.

"We could use some oven cleaner," Keely said meekly.

"Well, go ahead and take my Blazer," he said, relenting. "You don't need to waste money on a cab."

Keely nearly dropped the phone. For Tyler to offer his Blazer was so rare that she couldn't believe her ears. "You'll let me drive the Blazer?"

"Yes, but be careful with it. I just had it washed yesterday. Be sure and park it away from all those clowns who get out and bang their doors into it, and don't take it down muddy roads, don't curb the white walls—"

"Do you want me to put it into my purse and carry it into the store with me?"

"No," he replied patiently. "I just don't want you horsing around through a bunch of mudholes or coming home with dents in the side of it."

"I don't 'horse' around with my own car or drive it through mudholes. Why would I do that to . . . ?" Her voice trailed off contemplatively.

"Oh, hell, I hope I haven't given you any ideas." He groaned.

"I'll take good care of your car." She dismissed his response hurriedly. "And, Ty, I'll be happy to go for a ride with you after I get home."

"All right, I'll even throw in dinner," Tyler said, his voice perking up. "What time will you be back."

"I should be back by five."

"Good, see you then. Oh, and Keely . . . I'm looking forward to tonight," he said in an intimate tone.

"So am I." Keely's voice softened. "Why couldn't you have been this nice when we were married."

"Did you get a divorce since I left this morning?"

"No, I meant when were were really married."

"As far as I know, we are 'really' married," Tyler said curtly. "I've got to get off the phone, Keely. Take good care of the Blazer."

"I will." Keely replaced the receiver in the hook carefully. When Mr. Jerico saw his wife this evening, he was going to see a miraculous change. He would simply love it!

What had seemed like a perfectly marvelous idea two hours ago now had shades of lunacy about it. The rhythmic snipping of the scissors made Keely a little uneasy as she saw the mounds of dark hair piling up on the floor next to her chair.

"I have women who would crawl on their hands and knees to China to have hair like yours," the operator said between snapping her gum and swiveling the chair Keely was sitting in in different directions. "How long has it been since you had it cut?"

"I don't remember the last time," Keely admitted, wincing as another cluster of curls hit the floor. "I usually have the ends trimmed once a year, but it's been at least six years since it was actually cut."

The vivacious blonde's dangling hoop earrings swung jauntily as she chattered nonstop, her scissors working rapidly. "Well, with the shape of your face, you can wear this new short style very easily." *Snip, snip, snip, snip.* "Well, what do you think?" Judy swung the chair back around to face the large mirror.

Keely thought she now looked like she was somewhere between the ages of twelve and fourteen years old! Good heavens! She had hoped to come out of this shearing with a look of sophistication and aplomb, like Sheila, and now look at her!

"It's different," she managed weakly, staring back at the strange image in the mirror.

"You're going to love it," Judy assured her as she turned on the blow dryer and reached for a round, metal-bristled brush. "So will your husband."

Keely's spirits picked up considerably. That had to be true; Tyler *was* going to love it! After all, it did look

97

exactly like Sheila's now—sexy, swingy, and bouncy. Perhaps for the first time, Keely let her mind explore the possibility of reconciliation with her husband. Would it be possible for her to win his love back? She knew that there were still multitudes of problems between them, but if they both really applied themselves to the situation, couldn't they save their marriage? Chris had said the night before that it all came down to whether one person loved another person enough to try to overcome the obstacles. Well, she had no doubt that she loved Tyler enough to fight for him, and by the way he had acted this morning, maybe, just maybe, he might be willing to try again. For Keely it would be a matter of holding her temper and being more aware of Tyler's needs for love and security. For Tyler it would be a matter of trust. Could he trust in her love and never doubt her loyalty to him again? Keely didn't know, but she did know that it was worth at least a try.

It was only a little after four when Keely returned to the apartment. Deciding to go all out for her date with Tyler, she took a bath and put on one of the new dresses she had bought. The powder blue of the material made her eyes look misty and soft, and with her new hairstyle she presented a whole new image. Now that she had had a couple of hours to get used to it, she loved it. Gone was the girl who could never do anything right to please her husband! In her place now stood a woman of the world. He was going to go bananas when he saw what he was willing to give up so carelessly!

When she heard the click of his key, she straightened her dress, licked her lips so they would be shiny and inviting, and conjured up a sultry look on her face. She couldn't wait to see the look on *his* face. But his look, when it finally came, was not quite what she had expected.

"Holy . . . What did you do to your hair!" he thundered.

Keely nearly jumped back in fright from the menacing sound of his voice. For a minute she had the impression he didn't like her fashionable new haircut. Surely she was wrong. Licking her lips again, she smiled at him provocatively. "Do you like it?"

"Where's all your hair? That's a wig, isn't it?" he said with relief as he walked into the room and slammed the door shut. "Take it off; it looks like hell."

Keely's smile turned into a pout instantly. Marching over to the mirror, she reexamined her gorgeous new hairdo and demanded hotly, "What do you mean, it looks like . . . Tyler Jerico! This is the same hairstyle you think looks so hot on Sheila!"

"You mean to tell me that's *not* a wig and you actually had all that beautiful hair of yours cut off in that . . . that . . . punk haircut!" he roared.

"Punk haircut! How dare you!" she said through gritted teeth. "Are you telling me this hairstyle is good enough for your . . . your . . . Sheila, but it's not good enough for your wife?"

"Pardon me," he snapped back threateningly, both of them perilously close to ending the bet. "I don't remember *ever* implying to you one way or the other how I felt about Sheila's hairstyle. I *do* seem to remember telling you specifically on numerous occasions that I loved your hair the way it was and warned you not to ever cut it!"

"You are not my boss," she said through clenched teeth. Their two noses were nearly touching now, and their concentration on the touchy discussion was absolute. "And if I want to *shave* my head, it is none of your business, so bug off, mister!"

"You did this to win the bet, didn't you?" Tyler backed away from her slowly, his eyes flashing in outrage. "And I was beginning to think you had changed. Well, it's not going to work, Keely. You're not making me lose my temper over this little act of independence." He backed off entirely, gaining control of his emotions rapidly.

"Win the bet! I certainly did not cut my hair to win that stupid bet! I cut it . . . I cut it because I was sick of looking

99

like a teenybopper!" She would swallow her tongue before she would tell him she cut it to look better for him!

"Well, you've failed miserably," he snapped back. "I'd be afraid to drive down the street with you now. The cops would pick me up for trying to molest a minor!"

"You're the most impossible man I have ever had to deal with in my life!" Keely whirled on her heel and headed for the bedroom with a militant stride. When she reached the door and started to slam it with full force, Tyler's calm voice reached her. "You slam that door—I win the bet."

Her hand gripped the doorknob tightly. Was it worth the effort to try to stay in this house another three days with him, or should she do what he was aching to do— slam the door so hard it would fall off its hinges. She glanced up and caught Tyler's eyes sparking with the look of victory. Taking a deep, cleansing breath, her hand closed around the doorknob and pulled the door quietly shut. She was not going to be the one who lost this bet!

An hour later Tyler knocked on the bedroom door and said in a curt voice. "Get your rear in gear if you're going with me!"

Keely had been standing by the window, gazing out at the mountains, wondering how she could have ever given serious thought to reconciliation with that moron. "Thanks for the lovely invitation, but I think I'll stay here," she crooned.

"Suit yourself, but there's nothing in the house to eat," he warned her.

Keely's stomach rumbled. Her meals had been coming few and far between lately, and she didn't relish the thought of going to bed on an empty stomach. Why should she suffer when he obviously was going to go stuff his face! "Tyler, wait a minute, I'm going!" She grabbed her sweater and ran out of the bedroom.

As they walked through the garage, she saw his eyes checking over the Blazer discreetly.

"I haven't put one dent in it . . ." she said coldly as she opened the door of the red sports car, "or gotten one drop of mud on your precious toy."

"I didn't say you did," he returned blandly as he climbed in the driver's side.

"Your eyes said I did."

"Your voice said you were mad last night, but you said that didn't count, so whatever my eyes say shouldn't concern you now." He started the car with a roar. "Where do you want to eat?"

"Let's just drive around until we see something appealing," she heckled, feeling very out of sorts.

"Let's don't. We'll go to a steakhouse."

"Then why ask?"

He brought his face around to meet hers, ready to come back with a sharp reply, when he stopped and frowned. She sat silently and watched him study her, wondering what he was going to do. Reaching out, he cupped her chin, turning it from angle to angle. "Now that I really look at it, it doesn't look so bad."

"Don't you think she got one side a little too short?" Keely asked worriedly.

Tyler tipped her head more toward the light. "No, it looks even to me."

"It's going to be much easier to take care of," she assured him. "You don't think the left side looks shorter?" To her, it did.

He turned her head to the left side and studied it a moment. "No, it's even."

"Thank goodness," Keely sighed in relief. "I've been worried ever since I left the beauty shop."

Tyler put the car in gear and backed out of the garage. "You sure there's nowhere in particular you'd like to eat?"

"No, steak sounds fine to me," she agreed accommodatingly.

"Then steak it is." He looked over at her and winked broadly.

Steak was an excellent choice, and when they came out of the restaurant an hour later, they both felt in a much better mood. Driving along Pikes Peak Avenue, the awesome sight of the mountain stretched out before them. Tyler glanced over at her and grinned. "Are you still mad at me, or would you like to drive to the top of the mountain?"

"I'm not mad at you," she said with embarrassment, remembering her near fit earlier. "I'd like to see the top of it." They were so close in the small car that a very pleasing intimacy had developed since they left the restaurant.

"If I still had that old car we had when we first got married, I'd invite you to scoot over closer to me so you could hear better," he teased, "but I'm afraid the gearshift would be a little uncomfortable in this one."

Keely blushed shyly, remembering all the times she had nearly sat in his lap as they drove together, stealing heated kisses along the way.

"I'm comfortable where I am," she said primly, also wishing that they were in the other car.

"Next time we'll bring the Blazer," he promised in a sexy voice. "It has a bench seat."

The little car sped through town, quietly drawing closer to the mountain before them. As they began the long climb upward, Tyler told her that she would love to be here on the Fourth of July when the town had its annual Pike's Peak Hill Climb. The race up the mountain attracted famous drivers from all over, including the famous Unser brothers race team.

"People actually race up this road?" Keely asked in awe as the small car climbed the steep hill going no more than twenty miles per hour.

"They sure do, and love every minute of it," Tyler answered. "New Year's Eve is something you don't want to miss either. They put on a fireworks display at the top of Pikes Peak that literally lights up the sky."

102

"It sounds lovely," Keely said poignantly, realizing that she wouldn't be here to witness that event.

When they reached the top of the mountain, it was cold and windy. Keely could barely see the outline of the snow-crowned mountains that lay to the west. Tyler stopped the car, and they got out in the cold dark night and stood peering out into the darkness.

"How far up are we?" Keely asked, feeling very small and alone at the moment.

"Fourteen thousand, one hundred and ten feet. High enough for you?"

"It'll do," she said, shivering and snuggling down deeper into her thin sweater.

"You cold?" he asked, noticing her chattering teeth for the first time.

"A little. I should have brought a heavier wrap."

Tyler leaned back against the car and held his arms out to her, smiling. "Come here."

"That's not necessary," she protested as his arms reached out and drew her into the folds of his heavy sheepskin coat, wrapping it tightly around both of them. The feel of his muscular body molded tightly to hers made her pulse thud rapidly and her knees turn to jelly.

"Now, isn't this better? I'm not going to bite you," he murmured as he nuzzled her neck affectionately.

The wind whistled eerily as Keely pressed in closer to the warmth of his body, no longer caring whether it was proper or not. Hang propriety!

"I didn't want to leave you this morning, Keely," he whispered abruptly, his breath warm on her ear. "All I could think about at work today was getting back home to you tonight."

"I'm sorry I upset you with my hair," she whispered softly. "I honestly didn't do it to make you mad. Why do we always have to fight?"

He let out a long, audible sigh. "I wish I knew. When I met you, I thought I had found everything I ever wanted.

For the first time in my life, I had something that was mine; someone who loved me because they wanted to, not because they felt they had to."

Keely closed her eyes painfully, realizing that Tyler was finally talking to her about his childhood.

"After we broke up, I actually thought I was going to die, Keely. All the other times in my life when I had to leave a home or a particular set of parents I liked, I had experienced a certain amount of loneliness, but nothing like the feeling I had when I'd wake up in the middle of the night and reach over on your side of the bed and it would be empty. It was as if part of me had died and the other part was forced to go on living."

"I know. I had those same feelings. Only I would wake up, and I would be so scared. For the first time in my life I had lost something that I loved as much as my own life. When my mother died, I grieved, but it wasn't the same, Ty. I would sometimes lie for hours at night, needing you so badly that I ached, wanting you to be there to tell me everything was going to be all right and that everything that had happened was just a bad dream."

"The sad thing is, Keely, I think I knew from the day I married you I was going to lose you." She felt his arms tightening possessively around her waist.

"Why?" she asked gently. "Why would you think that? I loved you."

"I had lost everything that I ever loved in my life. Why would you be any different? I think that after I married you I turned slightly paranoid, worrying constantly if I was going to lose you. I used to pick at the smallest incident, trying to get the inevitable over with. Isn't that crazy? I loved you so much it hurt, yet I was hell-bent on destroying our marriage and getting all the pain and hurt over with. My only problem was, it never left. It only grew stronger."

Keely turned in his arms, the strong wind whipping her short hair about her face in wild disarray. Her arms came up shyly around his neck, and her eyes were gentle and contemplative. "It wasn't all your fault. I was short-tempered and hard to get along with at times. Even though I loved you, you could make me forget all reason when you'd start accusing me of flirting with other men, or implying there was something fishy going on between Craig and me. It suddenly occurred to me last night at the Morgans that maybe I hadn't taken the extra time to show you how much I did love you. I should have realized that with your childhood you might have needed more assurance of my love than what I was giving."

Tyler's body stiffened in resentment. "I'm not some emotional cripple who needs handling with kid gloves," he said defensively. "Sure, I didn't have a permanent home, but I made out all right."

"I wasn't suggesting that at all," Keely said patiently. "I only meant that I think I understand you better now than I did then."

His eyes clung to hers as he pulled her in tighter to his thighs, his hands holding her just under her rib cage gently. "Every time you got mad at me when I mentioned Craig, it only fed my doubts and suspicions about the two of you. I knew in my heart you loved me, and I *do* believe you when you say it was all my imagination, but—" His voice broke off raggedly.

"But, what?" she asked tenderly, reaching up to brush a lock of his flying hair out of his eyes. The wind was blowing so hard they could barely hear each other now.

"But, the fact is, I'm still the same old Tyler, and, no matter what, I will always be jealous and overly possessive of you. You deserve a man who can give you more than that."

Her faint smile had a touch of sadness. "Are you saying you don't think we can ever work out our problems, Tyler?"

"I don't know, Keely. I honestly don't know."

There was a gentle softness to her voice as her eyes

traveled over his face, loving every tired line, every crease, every feature that composed the countenance of the man she loved. "Don't you think I should be the one to decide what I should have in a man? Maybe I don't want a man who wouldn't be just a little jealous and possessive of me. Now, you notice I did say 'just a little.' "

A tiny grin hovered at the corner of his mouth. "You think I overdo it a bit, huh?"

"A bit," she admitted dryly.

His hands slipped up her arms, bringing her closer. "Do you know something, Mrs. Jerico? This time I'm not going to ask if I can kiss my wife. There wouldn't be a force here on earth powerful enough to stop me right now," he said hoarsely as his mouth slowly descended to meet hers. The familiar touch of his lips on hers sent shock waves through her entire body. In one lurching motion forward, she was returning his kiss with a hunger that had burned within her for six long, unbearable months, caring not the least bit about what he would think of her response. She was a woman dying of thirst, and he was her oasis. She was not ashamed to drink deeply. His fingers slid sensuously over her arm as his mouth moved over hers, devouring its softness. What had ever made her think she would be able to live without this man? That would be sheer madness, and at that moment, Keely knew without a doubt that she would always love Tyler Jerico. For better or for worse.

He broke off the kiss and buried his face in her hair, whispering, "I've dreamed of kissing you like that every night we've been apart. I used to lie in bed in the dark and try to remember the feel of your lips on mine, the way your hair always smelled like wildflowers, the way your fingers used to feel when they touched my skin . . ." His mouth took hers again with a savage intensity as his hands explored the soft lines of her back, her waist, her hips, molding her to his body. Love flowed like warm honey from her as she returned his kiss with abandon, wanting nothing more than to stay locked in his arms forever. Too soon, his lips left hers, and he buried her face in his broad chest, his ragged breathing slowing to a normal rate after a few moments. Only the sound of the wind could be heard on the top of the mountain as Keely lay limp in his arms. Neither one wanted to break the silence or the magic that had just taken place between them. It was several minutes before he finally loosened his hold on her, saying gently, "It's getting colder, let's go home."

They drove back home in complete silence. Keely stared out at the passing streetlights, her mind whirling in confusion. Tyler had not said the words, but she knew how badly he needed her tonight. Didn't she need him just as much? It had been a long time since she had felt his touch. There had been no other man for her since him, and her need was as strong as his. There had been times when that need had been a raw ache, a pain so strong that her nights had been spent tossing and turning for hours before she was able to lose herself in the oblivion of sleep. They were still married. Why would it be wrong for her to let her defenses down for just one night? *Because, you dummy, he just told you he didn't think you and he could ever work out your problems,* a small nagging voice echoed through her head. *He probably hasn't been celibate for these last six months,* it persisted. Sheila had undoubtedly kept him from tossing and turning at night. That was another thing that was beginning to worry her. Sheila hadn't called or come around since she came to the apartment the other night. Apparently Tyler had warned her about the bet and asked her to stay away until Keely was on her way back home with the divorce papers signed in his favor!

As Tyler was putting the car away in the garage, Keely rushed into the bathroom and showered quickly. By the time Tyler was ready for his shower, she was out, brushing her short hair in front of the mirror.

"You through in here?" he said, sticking his head in the steamy room, grinning deviously as he saw the way she frowned when the brush couldn't find anything to grip. "You still like your short haircut?"

"It's going to take some getting used to," she admitted dryly. "I'm through. You can have the shower."

"Hey," he said tenderly as she brushed past him on her way out, "I'm only teasing you. I think you look downright sexy with it cut like that."

"Of course, even if I do look like a man?" Keely asked resentfully. "Or does it remind you of Sheila's hair?"

Tyler stuck his lower lip out playfully. "Aw, c'mon, let me make you feel better."

"Take your shower," she said relentingly, letting out a breath. "I accept your dubious compliment."

Ten minutes later he turned out the light and got into bed. The room grew quiet as Keely lay on her side, hoping that he would reach over and draw her back into his arms. It was strangely silent on his side of the bed. She lay listening and waiting another few minutes, until she heard the sound of his even breathing, signaling that he had dropped off to sleep as easily as a child. Keely was outraged! After what had taken place between them earlier, he had the gall to get into bed and casually go to sleep without at least having the common decency to make a pass at her! Well, he wasn't going to get away with it! She picked up her pillow and slammed it down hard on his sleeping face. "Tyler!"

A deep laugh rumbled from his chest as he answered meekly, "Yes."

Keely sat up and glared at him in the dark. "You weren't asleep at all, were you?!"

"No, why?" he asked in mock surprise. "Did you think I was?"

"Oh, no," she lied as she lay back down to give him another opportunity to make an indecent suggestion to her. She'd no doubt turn him down flat after the outrageous way he had ignored her, but it would be comforting to know he had at least tried.

"Did you want something?" he asked solicitously.

"Who, me? No, of course not. I just wondered if you forgot to set the alarm."

"You have such a gentle way of getting my attention," he said with mock affection. "No, I didn't forget to set it. You're sure you didn't want anything else?"

That nincompoop was going to make it hard for her! "No . . . yes," she said in a small voice.

"Good, I just wanted to be sure we were on the same wavelength," he said, grinning tenderly.

"Oh, Tyler, I want you so much," she sobbed, falling into his arms even before he finished speaking.

His hand slid across her silken belly and he groaned softly. Her body melted against his as his mouth came down on hers hard and searching. Slowly his hands moved downward, skimming either side of her body to her thighs, kissing her hungrily. "Oh, Keely, my Keely!" was all he could murmur as their mouths mutually devoured each other. She felt the passion rising in her, clouding her brain, filling her world with nothing but the man holding her. He rolled over, pinning her beneath him as he forced her lips open with his thrusting tongue. His tormented moan was an open invitation for Keely to familiarize herself with every inch of his body once again. His lips left her mouth to move down to touch a nipple with tantalizing possessiveness. "Oh, damn, how I've missed you," he rasped as his mouth came back up to plunder the softness of hers.

Their bodies surged closer to each other, their hands groping wildly for each other's nearness. Six months had been a long time for Keely, of being deprived of the taste and feel of her husband, of the agonizingly sweet way his hair-rough form met and molded so perfectly with the softness of hers.

"I didn't think you wanted me . . . you were going to sleep. . . ." Her hands touched his shoulders, moving down to stroke his back as she matched his ardent kisses.

"I want you. I had to hear you say you wanted me.

. . ." His mouth left her lips to trail down the length of her slender frame once more, placing moist kisses near her navel. "Say it again, Keely. Say you want me."

"I want you, Tyler," she whispered breathlessly as she writhed under the assault his mouth was making and he continued to work his way down her thighs heatedly.

She gasped in sweet agony, and they both knew that they would be unable to take the time to explore, to arouse a slow and titillating pleasure. It had been too long since they had been together, and they yielded willingly to the hunger that had been building for months within them. Grasping her hips tightly, he brought her up to meet him. Their bodies, in exquisite harmony with each other, soared together until the peak of delight was reached and their world shattered into a million stars.

Contentment and peace flowed between them as they drifted slowly back to earth. Lying side by side, their bodies naked and still moist from their lovemaking, they gently stroked each other's bare skin, reluctant for their passion to ebb.

"Well, what do you think, Sam," Tyler murmured dreamily in her ear, still determined to tease her about her haircut, even after what they had just shared.

"About what?" she murmured back sleepily, ignoring his taunt.

"About this waterbed theory. Was what just happened sheer dynamite, or was it the waterbed that made it so terrific, or was it merely that I was a hungry man?"

Keely cocked one eye open. "*Were* you a hungry man?"

"Sure I was." His voice sounded serious.

"Tyler, are you lying to me?"

"You remember that two-hundred-fifty-pound woman wrestler we saw on TV last night? The one with the mustache?"

"Yes."

"Even she was beginning to look good to me!"

Keely punched him disbelievingly. "Be serious!"

110

"Now, before you get nasty, just take my word for it. *I was a hungry man.*" He laughed softly.

Keely hugged his neck tightly. "Aren't you going to ask me if I was hungry?"

"Are you kidding?" he asked, arching both of his brows comically. "I'd say you must have just come through a famine!"

"You louse!" She hit him with her pillow. "Couldn't you humor me a little?"

"I don't want to humor you," he said, moving his body over hers once more. "I want to make love to you again," he whispered suggestively against her mouth.

"Surviving a famine isn't easy," she agreed as his mouth closed over hers. "Perhaps I should start planning for the next drought."

"Perhaps we both should," he agreed amicably as his hand reached down and stroked her intimately. "You wouldn't think me a sex-starved old man if I—"

His words were cut short as Keely reclaimed his mouth coaxingly. With graceful ease she slid sensuously on top of his muscular chest, her tongue mingling sweetly with his.

"This time, do you think we could take it a little slower, 'old man,' " she asked between slow, languid kisses.

"That will be entirely up to you, Mrs. Jerico," he replied in a suggestive voice. "If you start . . . Keely!"

"Tyler!" she mocked as her fingers tickled lightly down his rib cage and wandered on toward his hips with tantalizing slowness.

"Didn't your mother ever tell you nice girls don't do the things you're doing?" His breath caught for a moment as she reached her ultimate goal.

"I believe she did mention it a couple of times. But, I'm sure she didn't say a thing about this." Her mouth played teasingly along his navel, kissing the hairline that ran enticingly lower.

An urgent, sexy growl rumbled deep in Tyler's throat

as he pulled her mouth back up to meet his quickly. "If you want me to take it slow, you're going to have to stop that!" he warned.

Their kisses became tender, each one increasing in intensity until he rolled over with her still locked tightly in his arms and smothered her lips with demanding mastery.

Once again time lost all meaning as he entered her, then paused for a moment, his hand coming up to trace his fingertips lightly across her lips. "Is this slow enough, ma'am," he grinned wickedly, lying motionless now.

"If it were any slower, you'd have to wake me when it's over," she grinned back. "Are you going to tease, or are you going to be serious?"

"Serious, I think," he replied solemnly after a moment of consideration. He brought his mouth back to hers persuasively. "Very serious, ma'am."

Within moments their passion was pure and highly explosive, sending them once more soaring on the floodtide of shuddering ecstasy.

Much, much later, as they were both drifting off to sleep in each other's arms, Keely fought the terrible feeling of depression that began to settle over her. Not once during their lovemaking had he asked for a reconciliation between them, or offered to call off their silly bet. If he actually did want to go through with the divorce, she didn't know how she would face that prospect. But the choice was not hers now. From now on, the ball would be in Tyler's court.

Tyler was still awake long after he heard Keely's quiet breathing as she dropped off to sleep in the cradle of his arms. How many times had he had to bite back the words to call off their silly wager tonight? But she hadn't said anything about the bet, so she must be willing to go on with the divorce. Well, if she still wanted the divorce, he wouldn't stand in her way. She had every right to find a man she could live in harmony with. Even though she had

112

no feelings for Craig, Tyler knew that Craig would give his eye teeth for her, and he would be there to pick up the pieces after the divorce became final. Tyler pulled his wife closer in his arms, breathing in the soft fragrance of her body.

Dear God, how he loved this woman. But from now on it would be up to her if the divorce papers were signed or not. It was out of his hands. With that thought, he unknowingly had returned the ball straight back to her court. Game point!

CHAPTER SEVEN

A vague feeling of depression still lingered with Keely the following morning. Only two more days, and the bet would expire. At the moment they were at an impasse, so Keely was going to have to take the bull by the horns and do something drastic. Last night had been wonderful, something she had dreamed of for many long months, but now, in the light of morning, she had to face cold reality. Tyler did not love her enough to cancel the bet, or the cursed divorce proceedings. It was perfectly obvious he still was sexually attracted to her. He surely couldn't have faked what had transpired between them last night. Well, maybe he had to concentrate a little harder on the last two times they had made love toward early morning, but she *knew* his heart had been in it the other two times! Now she mused thoughtfully as she picked up her coffee cup and walked over to the kitchen window. Her mission was coming down to the final tedious stages. Up until today she really hadn't applied her full potential to this dilemma. Keely sighed softly as she gazed out at the beautiful fall morning. She didn't want the divorce. She was very tired of kidding herself and trying to keep up the facade of making herself believe that she did want it. She had always loved Tyler, and after last night that love burned stronger than ever.

An idea began to form in her mind slowly. Maybe she should make one last, desperate try at winning his love back, *and* getting him to call off the wager, before she devoted herself entirely to lowering the boom on him. Now, what was Tyler's weakest link? Well, his second weakest link? After living with him over a year, she *knew* his weakest link, and after last night . . . She stared out the window, an idea teasing her lightly. No! She simply couldn't. He would see through her plan in a minute, and laugh her right out of town. But, on the other hand, if it worked, and he saw what a desirable, loving wife he was willing to let slip through his fingers, wouldn't it be worth the chance?

She crossed the room to the telephone and picked up the directory lying beneath it. If she could find a costume shop, she would do it! It was going to be a long shot, but what the heck. The most she could do was make him mad, and if that occurred, it would be to her advantage also! Tyler did not realize what a genius he was dealing with! He would be so overcome by desire for her, he would literally be down on his knees begging for another chance.

The scene was set; the wine was poured; the lights were lowered. Keely stood in front of the mirror, nervously adjusting her veils. This was sheer madness, and as the time drew closer for Tyler to arrive home from work, she grew more apprehensive. If this failed, she was going to be mortified—to say the least! Glancing down at her bare navel, she groaned. This costume was unbelievable. If she hurried, she would have time to take it off, put her jeans back on, pick up the pillows on the living room floor . . .

The sound of Tyler coming in through the front door interrupted her thoughts. Darn it! She was cornered like a rat.

"Keely?" Tyler was standing in the doorway, squinting through the dark room. "What in the hell's wrong with the lights?"

With grim determination, Keely reached over and flipped on the record player. The sultry sounds of lutes and tambourines filled the air seductively.

"Come in, darling."

Tyler stood at the door, his hands on his hips, trying to figure out why there were only candles burning in the room. Keely floated across the room to greet him, her veils and a cloud of alluring perfume wafting ahead of her. She paused before him and reached out to encircle his neck with her arms. The jangle of her many gold bracelets sounded provocative in the stillness that had now overtaken the small apartment.

"Where's Keely?" Tyler breathed in a husky voice as he put a large hand to her bare midriff and pulled her close to his tall, athletic frame.

"Who?" she asked innocently, bringing his mouth down to meet hers enticingly. Her lips feather-touched his with tantalizing persuasion.

"Keely, my wife." His tongue sent shivers of desire racing through her as he picked her up and pressed her tightly against the length of his body and moved into the room, closing the door firmly behind him. He pitched his jacket over toward the couch and continued holding her close.

"I'm afraid I don't know any Keely, sir. I'm just a poor servant girl who has been sent here to dance for you . . . please you, in any way that you so desire," she whispered, kissing his chin, then moving on to touch his ear moistly with her tongue.

"No kidding," he breathed hotly against the swell of her breasts, his mouth nibbling its way deeper. "What's your name, little servant girl?"

"It does not matter, sir," she said in a breathlessly alluring voice. "Are you willing to let me . . . serve you?

116

I mean, I would not wish to cause any trouble between you and your wife." Her lips nibbled at his earlobes as he became fully aroused, holding her closer to the undeniable evidence of his passion.

"Oh, you won't," he assured lazily as his hands worked their way beneath the layer of gauzy veils and found more bare skin. He stroked her velvety softness with a smooth easiness, a bright flare of desire building steadily in his smoky gaze.

"That's good," she murmured throatily as a spurt of hungry desire spiraled helplessly through her. "I am here *only* to please," she reminded him again as she buried her hands in the thickness of his hair.

"Well, shy little servant girl, you have my permission to start 'pleasing' any time you want to," he urged.

"Is there a hurry, kind sir?" Her lids slipped down over her eyes and she inhaled his delightful scent.

"You might say that," he agreed, pressing up against her boldly. "You know, shy little servant girl, this is something every man dreams about. What have I done to deserve all this?"

They exchanged a smoldering kiss, the touch of his lips filling her with a delicious, heady sensation.

She shrugged her shoulders and replied in a silky voice, "You are *very* deserving, sir. Any woman would deem it an honor to . . . serve you."

Their mouths merged again for a moment before she pulled away and buried her face in the strong column of his neck.

"But I *do* hate to think about your . . . lovely . . . wife," she persisted.

"Really. Why?"

Keely tensed slightly at his aloof manner. True, this was only a silly game, but did he have to act *so* disinterested?

"Well, you know, if she should find out . . ."

"Oh, don't worry about her, we're getting a divorce anyway," he consoled her as he eased the silky material

117

of her halter aside and began to fondle one soft globe, placing slow, moist kisses around the small pink bud.

"Oh, my!" Keely gasped as his mouth fully covered it now and sucked gently. "Does your wife no longer please you?" she squeaked.

"No, she really doesn't," he replied matter-of-factly. His mouth traveled back up to capture hers in a possessive kiss. Her soft curves molded to the contours of his body as she stood on tiptoe and surged intimately against him.

If she were smart, she knew she should let the conversation drop right now and proceed with her plans.

"Why?"

"Why, what?" he asked between unhurried kisses.

"Why doesn't your wife please you?"

"You know, you talk an awful lot for a shy servant girl who has been sent to please me," he pointed out as his breathing became increasingly labored. "Can't we discuss my wife some other time?"

"No," she insisted, trying to catch her breath from his overpowering virile assault on her senses. "What's wrong with your wife? Is she ugly, fat, undesirable?"

Tyler buried his face in the fragrance of her hair and whispered softly, "Um . . . well, let's see, she's about five-two, weighs around a hundred pounds; she has eyes the color of a robin's egg, hair, what there is of it, the color of rich chocolate. No, she's fairly cute, even if she does look a lot like a boy now."

"Tyler, that's not funny!" Keely was close to becoming piqued.

"Now, hold on, little servant girl, why should you care about my wife? You know you could put a real damper on a man's sex life by constantly referring to his wife while he's trying to . . . to . . . be pleased," he said in a petulant tone.

"Why is it all men think that in order to be sexy a woman has to wear her hair down to her waist and poofed out like a wild woman's?" she asked irritably, pushing back from his ardent embrace. "You sure never say anything about Sheila's hair!"

"You're right; I don't. Why do *you* keep bringing it up?" He walked over to the bar and tripped on the mound of pillows she had placed strategically on the floor. She had planned to have him sit down in the middle of them and watch her dance a very lustful and arousing belly dance. "What are all the pillows doing in the middle of the floor?" he snapped. "I nearly broke my neck!"

"I was . . . cleaning house, and I haven't had time to put them back yet!" she replied, peeved. Brother! She had known this idea was doomed to failure from the very beginning. One simply could not be nice to a jackass!

Tyler poured a Scotch and water then downed it in one quick swallow. He reached over and blew out the two small candles that were burning next to the bar and flipped on the lamp. "Now, you want to tell me what this little harem scene is all about."

"I don't know what you're talking about," she muttered, twisting her veil in a knot nervously.

He looked at her ironically. "You mean this is the way you go around the house normally." His voice literally dripped with sarcasm.

"I've been invited to a costume party when I get back home," she improvised haughtily. "I was only trying on my costume."

"In that skimpy thing! With *whom*?"

Keely's temper flared. "None of your business."

"I thought you said you weren't seeing Craig again."

"Who said anything about Craig? Do you think Craig is the only man in town?"

"I thought," he enunciated clearly, "that you implied last night you were not seeing anyone at the present."

"I implied I was not *sleeping* with anyone . . . at the present!" Let him think what he wanted! He would anyway.

Tyler's eyes narrowed dangerously. "I'm sorry. I

misunderstood you." He walked over to the sofa and picked up his discarded jacket. "I just came home to pack an overnight bag."

"Where are you going?" she asked resentfully.

"I've got to go out of town to a construction site. I'll be gone overnight." In a few minutes he came back in the room with a small bag. "I'm going to take a cab to the airport. Can you pick me up at the office tomorrow evening?" he asked coolly.

"I suppose so." She had twisted her lovely veils into a mangled mess.

"You better get that garb off before you shred it to pieces," he growled as he stalked to the door.

"Tyler!" Keely jumped up from the couch and followed him to the door. "Tyler, I didn't mean for us to get in another argument." Here they were, mad at each other again.

"Keely," he groaned, reaching out and touching her chin with one long finger.

"You could call the bet off," she said urgently. "It's this darn bet that makes us so tense with each other," she rushed on, praying that he would say the words she longed to hear.

"If you want to call the bet off, you do it." His eyes were dead serious now as he captured hers. He was giving her every opportunity. All she had to say was yes, she would call the bet off, and he would get down on his knees and beg her for a reconciliation.

Keely stared back into the troubled depths of his eyes, and her voice came out very small and timid. "No, you'll have to call it off. I won't." She would never be sure of his love if he weren't the one to cancel the wager.

"I'm not calling it off, Keely," he said gently.

"Then so be it," she whispered.

"Pick me up around five tomorrow," he said with a tired sigh, then grabbed up his suitcase. "Don't be late, and be careful with the Blazer."

She had to smother the desire to laugh hysterically. Don't be late? It seems that she was already too late. Too late to save her troubled marriage. "I won't be late, and I'll guard the Blazer with my life."

He stole one last glance at his wife standing forlorn in the middle of the room. He wanted to take her in his arms so badly and kiss away that painful look from her youthful face. His hands clasped in tight fists as he fought the powerful force invading his body. No, *she* had to be the one. With one last glance he closed the door between them and walked out into the dark night.

Keely spent another miserable night. It was funny how she had only slept in Tyler's bed two nights, but already she felt blue and all alone by herself in the big bed. It had been very comforting to reach out in the night and feel him there beside her. Even if she didn't touch him, she knew he was there. How would she bear the loneliness when she returned home? Maybe she should start considering another man in her life. Anything would be better than the terrible lonely nights spent in solitude. A good book, a TV show, a talk with a friend on the telephone, all served their purposes, but they could never take the place of another person lying beside you at night, a man who loved and cared only for you.

Keely awoke in the morning feeling tired and grouchy. The clock had ticked off yet another day, and tomorrow she would go home. They still hadn't decided what would happen if neither one lost the bet. At the rate they were going, it was going to be a dead even finish. They would simply have to split up the community property as they planned in the first place and be satisfied with that arrangement. She would have bet her life that he would never have made it as far as he had, but he was full of surprises.

The phone rang as she finished making up the bed. "Hello?"

"Hi, this is Pam Morgan."

"Hi, Pam." Keely sat down on the bed. "I've been meaning to call you and thank you for the lovely dinner. And to apologize for my bad behavior."

Pam's laughter rang out on the other end of the line. "Don't give it a thought. I know how these family squabbles can put you in a bad mood. Have you and Tyler got any plans tonight?"

"No, not that I know of, Pam. He's gone on a business trip, but he's supposed to return this evening."

"I know, Chris flew up to Wyoming with him. They took the company plane."

"Oh, I wasn't aware Tyler knew how to fly a plane."

"Sure he does. He got his license not long ago. Chris and I were wondering if you'd like to go out to dinner with us this evening. There's a great little place not far from the construction office that has good steaks."

"Gee, I don't know, Pam," Keely said thoughtfully. "I don't feel at liberty to accept invitations for Tyler anymore. I hope you understand."

"Of course I understand, but why don't I ask Tyler when I see him this afternoon. I'm going out to the airport to pick them up later on."

"If it's all right with him, it will be fine with me," Keely said sincerely. This would be their last night together, and she would like to spend it in tranquility with him—if such a feat were humanly possible.

"If he agrees, I guess we'll see you around seven," Pam said brightly.

"I'll be looking forward to it," Keely said politely. Replacing the phone on the hook carefully, she immediately regretted accepting the tentative invitation. Somehow, she wanted to spend their last evening alone. She felt she probably would never have an occasion to see Tyler again after she said good-bye to him tomorrow. The pain tugged at her heart once more as she went in to pack a few of her things. She had to get her mind off her problems. A weak

122

sun was trying to peek its head from beneath a thick layer of clouds. It had rained heavily during the night, and the air was cold and damp this morning. By noon Keely knew she would have to get out of the apartment or lose her mind. It was still hours before she was to pick Tyler up at his office, so she decided to take a drive up the mountain one more time. She wanted to see the view from the top of Pikes Peak in the daylight hours.

This time she dressed more warmly, taking one of Tyler's old coats along for extra warmth. The faint smell of his aftershave clung to the rough fabric, and her senses became alive and yearned for his touch as she backed the Blazer out of the garage. She wondered fleetingly if he would miss this jacket if she took it home with her. There was nothing left in her small apartment to remember him by. He had instructed her to pack everything he owned and ship it to him shortly after their heated separation, and she had been only too glad to oblige his request at the time. Now she wished she had cheated just a little and kept at least one small thing. For the next few hours Keely drove aimlessly around, her mind constantly going over and over the stormy marriage and reaching a deadend every time she sought some reasonable solution. There didn't seem to be any. It always came back to the simple question, did she want to be miserable with him, or without him?

She honestly didn't know. The only thing that was clear in her mind as she drove along the winding roads, barely taking note of the beautiful scenery surrounding her, was the fact that she loved the man beyond all reason. Would that be enough to base a marriage on? Certainly it was the main ingredient in a happy marriage, but would it see her through all the years of quarreling and bickering over trivial matters?

Keely glanced down at the needle hovering close to the empty mark on the gas gauge. She had better turn back and head for a gas station. By the clock on the dash, she

123

had a little over an hour before she was due at Tyler's office, and she didn't want to make him angry this last night they were together. She stifled a giggle as she realized her contradictory thoughts. One minute she was plotting how to get him mad, the next minute she was going out of her way to avoid the prospect.

Somehow she had gotten off on a dirt road, and she could hear what sounded like muddy gravel being thrown up against the side of the Blazer. The thought of bringing back Tyler's Blazer with even a hint of mud on it made her very uneasy, and she made a mental note to take it by the nearest car wash before she picked him up. She slowed down somewhat, and the sound diminished. There was no sense in making it muddier than it was already. She was going to have to find a place to turn around before long, and she pinned her hopes on finding such a place just over the small rise coming up. The thought had barely left her mind when a car came flying over the hill. Keely glanced up just in time to jerk the wheel sharply to the right, sending the Blazer careening off toward a steep ditch. She shut her eyes and stomped down on the brake, trying to bring the vehicle under control. The Blazer jumped most of the ditch but didn't quite make it, landing with one of the rear wheels wedged in the gully filled with muddy water. It came to rest against a barbed wire fence, which had left its calling card running down the entire length of the passenger side.

When the Blazer finally stopped, Keely sat holding her hands over her mouth in stunned apprehension. It had all happened so fast she hadn't had time to catch her breath. The two occupants of the other car brought their automobile to an abrupt halt and tumbled out of the car in a mad rush to get to the Blazer.

"Hey, lady, are you hurt?" A teenage boy stuck his head against the car window on Keely's side and pecked on the glass. "Hey, lady, can you hear me?"

Keely turned to face him, nodding mutely. "I can hear you!"

"Well, roll down your window," he pleaded excitedly.

"Oh . . . yes," Keely cranked down the window hurriedly.

"Gee whiz, lady, I'm sure sorry. No one hardly ever uses this road, so I wasn't being careful enough. Are you hurt?"

"No, I don't think so." Keely was shaking like an aspen leaf in the wind, but she didn't think that she was actually hurt.

"Boy, I think this thing's stuck tighter than a tick," the other boy said as he walked around the Blazer, shaking his head in consternation. "Shoot, and this thing's a four-wheel drive, ain't it?"

"Is it muddy?" Keely asked, jumping out of the car.

"Muddy!" The two boys looked at her as if she were deranged. "Yeah, it's muddy all right," they agreed in unison.

Keely let out a horrified gasp as she started walking around the car on shaky legs. When she came to the passenger's side, she moaned out loud. "He's going to kill me!"

"Who?" the boys asked in wide-eyed unison again.

It was one thing for Keely to try to make Tyler mad by bringing his Blazer back muddy, and she had to admit that the thought had crossed her mind a couple of times, but it was quite another thing to send him to prison for the rest of his life on first degree murder charges! He would lay her out clean as a whistle for destroying his Blazer, and she knew it!

"Do you think you guys can help me get it out of this ditch?" she asked, chewing on her bottom lip nervously. If she could just get it out of the ditch, she might be able to get it to a garage before they closed; then she could pick up Tyler in a cab. She would find a way to explain what had happened and have it fixed before he got a look at the damage. It was a long shot, but she was desperate!

"I think I've got a chain in the back of my car," the driver of the other car said. "Maybe I can pull you out if I stay out here on the road."

"Well, it's worth a try," Keely agreed, dusting the dried mud from her hands off on her jeans. "I'm going to have to hurry. I'm supposed to pick up my husband by five." Picking him *up* isn't exactly what she would be doing. More like picking him *off*—the ceiling!

"It won't take a second." The two boys ran back to their car, and within a few minutes they were back with a long, heavy logging chain.

"Okay, lady, now you get in, and Butch will push from behind. I think we can get it out with no problem." He cast a wary glance at the back wheel sunk in the mud up to its axle. "Imagine, getting a four-wheel drive stuck! Your husband will never believe this!" he said in awe.

"Oh, I think he will!" Keely said grimly as she climbed back behind the wheel. Well, so much for the theory that they might spend their last night together in harmony!

"All right. Now, when I yell at you, you press on the gas real easy and sort of rock the wheels out of the ditch," the boy instructed in a shout, then, "Butch, you push on the back bumper at the same time. Everybody got it?"

"Got it!" Butch and Keely answered in unison.

He climbed back in his car and gunned the motor. Keely hoped to heaven he didn't decide to let out on the clutch at that particular moment, or Tyler could be picking his front bumper up while he was still in Wyoming!

Gently the boy eased out on the clutch, and Keely heard the chain tighten. "Okay now, start giving it some gas!"

Keely pressed down on the gas pedal lightly, and she heard the wheels spinning, but the truck wasn't moving an inch.

"It's not working," she yelled. "You're going to have to pull harder!"

"Okay, hold on!"

The other car's engine revved louder, and the chain popped ominously on the front bumper, but the stubborn Blazer still refused to budge.

"Wait a minute," Keely shouted, tumbling back down out of the driver's side. "I'm going to help Butch push!"

"I don't think it's going to do any good," Butch told her with an air of pessimism. "This thing's stuck here till doomsday."

"Why don't you get in and see if you can rock it better than I can?" Keely suggested, refusing to accept his gloomy assessment of the situation. "I'll push for a while."

"A little ole thing like you. That's like a gnat trying to shove a boulder out of his way," Butch scoffed.

"I don't plan on trying to lift the truck out of the ditch by myself, Butch," she said patiently. "I'm only going to push while you give it gas."

"Well," he relented skeptically, "whatever you think. I still don't think we're going to be able to get it out. We'll probably have to call a tow truck, and it might not be able to budge it either."

Brother, she would sure hate to be fighting a war with this guy! Butch ambled back up to the seat of the Blazer, and the process of trying to get the vehicle out of the ditch began all over again.

Butch might not have had a very optimistic outlook on the situation, but he certainly had a lead foot when it came to pushing on the gas pedal. The wheels spun in a whirling frenzy, throwing mud from one end of Keely to the other. Between pushing, spitting, and cursing, she was ready to admit defeat. But five minutes later the stubborn rear wheel suddenly broke free, springing forth out of the ditch like a wild animal. Keely tumbled over into the mud uttering every vicious oath she could think of as the side of her head hit the muddy water. Sitting up and angrily spitting the vile-tasting water out of her mouth, she yelled at Butch to slow down! He was, in Tyler's words, horsing around with the muddy vehicle on the road, playing with the four-wheel drive like a child with a new toy.

"Park it!" she shouted in a most unladylike voice. Tyler would turn gray if he saw the way his truck was being taken care of at the moment.

By the time she was back on the road again, her nerves were frayed, and she was in a nasty mood. No longer could she hold on to the slim thread of hope she would be able to drop the Blazer by a garage. It was after five now, and she was a dead duck for sure!

It was dark by the time she pulled up in front of the construction firm. Easing the Blazer into the first parking spot she saw, she jumped out of the truck and ran into the building. If she played her cards right, she would start limping when she saw Tyler, and maybe he would think that she had been hurt in the accident and show some pity on her. Maybe Robert Redford would knock on her door tomorrow morning, too, she thought snidely as her feet flew up the set of stairs leading to Tyler's office.

Tyler and Chris were just coming out of their office when a ball of mud came flying around the corner at them.

"Hey . . . whoa . . ." Chris laughed holding out his arms to shield his suit from her muddy hands.

"Keely?" Tyler's mouth dropped open. "Where have you been? What's happened to you?"

"Oh, Tyler," she whined in a pitiful voice, "I've been in a terrible accident."

Chris looked at her with immediate concern. "Are you all right?"

"Where's the Blazer?" Tyler asked simultaneously.

Keely glared at Tyler. "Aren't you even going to ask if I'm hurt?"

"I can see you're not. Where's the Blazer!"

"It's parked out fron . . . but, Tyler, before you look at it, I think I should explain something." Her voice broke off meekly as he spun around and ran back into his office.

"What did you hit, a mud cyclone?" Chris grinned, his

128

eyes surveying her muddy face, clothes, and hair. There wasn't a clean spot on her.

"He's going to wring my neck," she predicted in a breathless voice. "I'm getting out of here."

"Keely!" Tyler's voice roared through the building. "Get your rear in here!"

"You better go in," Chris said, his face beaming in a silly grin. "I'll go with you for protection."

Keely dragged her feet, shuffling protectively behind Chris as they entered the small office. Tyler was hanging out of his open second-story window, his face a sickly gray as he surveyed what resembled his Blazer parked below.

"What did you *do* to my truck?" he asked in a small boy's voice.

"I—I didn't mean to. This other car came up over the hill, and I had to swerve—" she started.

"Where's the piece of side trim on the driver's side?" he interrupted rudely.

Keely came over to peer out the window beside him. "What's side trim?"

"It's that silver strip that runs down the side of the truck."

"Oh that," she said, dismissing the matter lightly, "I threw it away. It was dragging on the pavement, and I figured you would have to get a new one anyway when they fixed the scratch that the barbed wire fence made."

Tyler was beginning to look dangerous now.

"Well, hell's bells, Tyler, I nearly got killed. And look at me," she stepped back for him to take a good long look at her muddied body. "I had to get in the ditch and help push on the back of the truck so the other boy could tie that big long chain around your bumper. And *I* was the one who kept saying I thought we could get it out without the expense of calling a tow truck, even when Butch said it would be stuck till doomsday," she said in one long breath. "How can you stand there and act like I deliberately took your Blazer out and brought it back in this horrible condition, when I went *out* of my way," she said emphasizing with stabbing finger, "to take good care of it!"

Chris stood watching the scene before him in fascination, trying hard to stifle his snickering.

"Oh, hell! There's a scratch down the side of the Blazer under all that mud?" Tyler asked weakly, his eyes never leaving the street.

"All the way down the passenger side," Keely confirmed gravely, shaking her head. "Starting from the back, clear down to the front. It looks awful."

Tyler turned back around slowly, his eyes a total blank. "If you've done this to make me mad, Keely . . ."

"No! No. Now, Tyler, just calm yourself down. You have got to believe me when I say it was an accident. These things just happen in life. I swear I didn't do this to make you mad." She helped him over to a chair and sat him down. "Here, let me get you a glass of water; you look pale." She rushed over to the water cooler and drew him a cup of cold water. "Before I leave tomorrow, I'll take it to a garage, and I'll have them restore it to its original condition. Then I'll have them send the bill to me," she promised, patting him on the back consolingly.

"Are my spoke hubcaps still on?" he asked hopefully as he accepted the water she offered.

"Two of them still are."

"Oh, hell." He sat the cup of water down and stared at the floor in desolation.

"Cheer up, Tyler," Chris broke in. "I'm sure once the mud's washed off the Blazer, the damage will be small. Thank God Keely wasn't hurt."

"Yes," Keely said kneeling down beside Tyler, patting his leg affectionately. "Thank God I wasn't hurt!" she said seriously.

Tyler turned shell-shocked eyes in her direction. "Yes, thank God," he said dryly. "Well, I suppose I should get it home and get a closer look at the damage." He stood

130

up and glanced back out the window, his mouth dropping open for a second time.

"What's the matter now?" Keely asked, peering over his shoulder at the street below. Her blue eyes widened as she saw the large tow truck pull away from the curb with the muddy Blazer hooked to the back of it.

Chris let out a hoot of laughter and doubled over, slapping his leg in merriment. "Keely, you parked in a No Parking zone!"

"I did?" she mumbled sheepishly.

Tyler turned back from the window, the muscle working tightly in his jaw. "You did," he pronounced grimly.

She smiled feebly, "I didn't know it was a No Parking zone, honest!"

Taking her by the hand like an errant child, Tyler practically dragged her through the office, mumbling all the way. "Let's go home before I do something I may live to regret!"

"Hey," Chris called between spasms of laughter, "do you want me to take you home?"

"No!" Tyler shouted as they bounded down the stairs two at a time. "I want you to stop your damn gigglin'!"

When they reached the street, Tyler hailed a cab with a shrill whistle, shoving Keely in the back seat and climbed in after her. After giving the driver his address, he turned to face her. "If I *ever* find out you did this on purpose, I'm coming after you," he threatened in a grim voice.

Keely jerked her hand out of his hard grasp. "I knew you'd be upset!"

"Upset! That's putting it mildly!"

"I know in your mind you're ready to strangle me."

"No, in my mind, I *murdered* you in cold blood," he said bluntly, staring out his side of the car.

"You didn't!" Keely gasped in outright indignation.

Tyler turned back and smiled wickedly. "Oh, but I did!"

"You are a cold, uncaring brute," she said miserably.

131

"Any man who would think more of his car than he would the welfare of his wife is . . . is a heartless beast!"

"*If* I thought my wife had not deliberately destroyed something that I took great pride in just to win an asinine bet that we made, then I might view this situation differently, but apparently she is hell-bent on getting a set of divorce papers signed and is willing to go to any length to do it! Well, you'll get your damn papers signed, Keely. But it will be in the morning when you're packing to go home! I've come this far without losing my temper completely; I can surely make it a few more hours." His voice returned to a calm, husky timbre.

The cab pulled up in front of the apartment building and deposited its surly occupants.

"Give me some change; all I've got's a fifty-dollar bill," Tyler snapped as he started to pay the fare.

Keely reached for her purse, then swallowed hard; she glanced back up at him. "I left it in the Blazer."

Tyler groaned, then handed the driver a bill, asking hesitantly, "I don't suppose you have the change."

"Nope," the driver replied with a broad grin. When he drove away a few minutes later, his grin was even broader.

Tyler started up the walk, dragging Keely behind him. Shrugging off his bruising grip in exasperation, she walked ahead of him, holding her head proudly. She was going to make it one more day, if only to prove to him he wasn't as smart as he thought he was! When he opened the apartment door, she went in ahead of him, slamming the door shut in his face. Let him try to insinuate she had lost her temper, she fumed. *Just let him try!*

CHAPTER EIGHT

"Out of the goodness of my heart I'm going to ignore that little tantrum," Tyler said serenely as he unlocked the door a second time and let himself in the apartment.

"You don't have a heart," Keely tossed over her shoulder as she marched toward the bathroom.

"What did you say?"

"I said, I'm going to take a shower. Do you mind!"

"As a matter of fact, I do," he said, slamming his keys on the table. "I've had a long, tiring day, and I'm getting in the shower first."

"*You've* had a long tiring day!" Keely sniffed disdainfully. "At least you haven't wallowed around in a mudhole for two hours, trying to get some ungrateful nincompoop's Blazer out of a ditch." She emphasized "ungrateful nincompoop."

"*I* didn't put some 'ungrateful nincompoop's' Blazer *in* the ditch," he reminded her as he loosened his tie. "Only an idiot could get a four-wheel drive stuck in a ditch in the first place."

"I'm through talking about it," she announced flatly, and walked over to the sofa and unthinkingly started to sit down.

"Don't you dare sit down on that couch," Tyler warned ominously. His hands stopped unbuttoning his shirt, and he watched her warily. If that mudball sat on his couch, it would be ruined!

Keely looked up and met his uneasy eyes, her blue ones sparkling combatively. "Why not? Would that make you mad?"

He took a step closer to her. "Not any madder than you'd be when I made you sleep on it again tonight."

She stepped closer to him. "I was already planning on sleeping on it anyway, Tyler Jerico. I've had it up to here with you!" She made an irritable slash across her forehead with her hand. "You'll notice that I'm saying all of this in a perfectly reasonable tone of voice. But I want you to know that I think you are the most obstinate, asinine, unreasonable . . ."

". . . jackass, horse's rear, lame-brain," Tyler added, turning away from her flushed and muddied face in a bored manner. "I know, I know. I've heard it all before. How come you accepted a dinner invitation with Pam and Chris without asking me?" he asked, changing the subject as he walked toward the bathroom.

"I didn't," Keely muttered as she pulled out some newspapers from the magazine rack and spread them out on the floor to sit on. "I distinctly told Pam I couldn't accept an invitation for you!" She plopped down on the papers, spread-eagled, staring up at the ceiling tiredly. She never wanted to live through another day like this one. When she got home, the first thing she was going to do was burn her marriage license.

"Well," Tyler called through the open bathroom door, "they're expecting us to meet them around seven. Do you think you can get yourself presentable in that length of time. Your hair won't be any problem. After you wash it, you can comb it with a toothbrush."

Keely closed her eyes, trying to ignore his heckling manner. "I'm not hungry."

134

"You made the plans. You're going." Tyler slammed the bedroom door heatedly. Within seconds it opened back up and Tyler stuck his face out, smiling angelically. "My goodness, the door just slipped out of my hand. Sorry if the noise startled you, sweetie."

Keely continued to ignore him. Somehow the fight had all drained out of her, and she was suddenly very very tired. She lay staring at the swirls in the white textured ceiling, listening to Tyler boisterously whistling in the shower. She closed her eyes once more, knowing that this would be one of the last times she would hear that sound. Funny how such an insignificant thing as hearing him tweet a racy sailor's song could make a hard knot rise up in her throat. Especially in view of the fact that only a few minutes ago she had been telling him just how much he disgusted her.

Muddy drops started to roll down her face, and she didn't know whether to laugh or keep crying. Her body ached from the hard jolt of the Blazer hitting the ditch, and she sobbed softly when she thought of the ludicrous picture she must make lying in the middle of the floor. Her fashionable hairdo was very unfashionable at the moment and didn't stand a chance at impressing her husband, with her coated in all this mucky mess. No wonder Tyler would be glad to get rid of her. Not only did she argue with him continually, but she seemed to be a constant thorn in his side.

Within a few minutes she was sobbing hard, trying unsuccessfully to wipe the muddy streaks away before Tyler came out of the bathroom. She was so tired! So tired of loving him, yet knowing without a doubt he would never be hers again. Her eyes closed in weary resignation.

The bedroom door opened, and she heard Tyler call out that the shower was empty. Rising to her feet, she avoided looking in his direction as she walked through the bedroom into the bath. He was standing at his open closet door, selecting a pair of trousers, and barely noticed as she limped by.

If time had permitted, she would have loved to have taken a long bath to try to soak away some of the pain she was beginning to feel. But she needed to be soaked from head to toe, and she contented herself with standing under the hot, steamy water and letting the pressure from the showerhead swirl away the mud and grime from her fatigued body. When she finally forced herself to turn the tap off, she felt a bit more human. Drying herself with a thick white towel, she wrapped a smaller one around her wet hair and opened the bathroom door a crack to let some of the steam escape.

Tyler walked in a few minutes later, a towel still wrapped around his waist, and reached over to plug in his electric shaver. Keely tried to ignore his powerful chest and the surge of longing she experienced as she reached for the blow dryer. "Do you mind, Tyler? I'm not through in here yet." She gave him an uneasy glance as she turned the dryer on and picked up her styling brush.

"Yes, I do mind," he said above the buzz of the razor. "We're going to be late if we don't get a move on."

"I really wish you would go on without me," she said over the drone of the dryer. "All I want to do right now is go to bed."

Tyler laid the razor down and reached around her for his bottle of aftershave. He poured a small amount out into the palm of his hand, then replaced the cap on the bottle.

Splashing the musky-smelling lotion on his face, he squinted in her direction. His hands paused suddenly as he asked, "What's the matter with your shoulder?"

Keely peered back over her right shoulder and saw an large ugly bruise. "I thought my shoulder was getting awfully sore," she acknowledged faintly.

Tyler reached over and touched the dark spot gently

with one of his fingers. "Hell, Keely, you didn't tell me you were hurt!" he exclaimed softly.

"I didn't think I was until we got back home. I'm just now beginning to get sore." She switched off the dryer and looked in the mirror to assess quickly the rest of her body. There were several dark splotches starting to appear on her arms and shoulders.

His compassionate gray eyes met her tired blue ones in the glass as Tyler said lovingly, "If I'd had any idea that you really hurt yourself, I would have made you stop by the hospital. Let me help you slip some clothes on, and I'll take you over there right now."

"That's not necessary. I was just thrown around a bit when the Blazer hit the ditch. Other than being sore, I'll be fine."

He stepped behind her to examine the bruises tenderly. His large hands sent shivers along her spine as she stood frozen in place. "I'll be all right," she said again.

Her stomach fluttered as his arms slipped around her waist and pulled her back against his hard length. "I could wring your neck for not telling me about this," he scolded tenderly.

"I honestly didn't know, Tyler." Her blue eyes pleaded with him not to start another argument. "Couldn't we please call a truce for this evening. This is our last night together, Ty. Can't we try to make it a happy one?"

A swift stab of pain crossed his handsome features as his eyes caressed hers, still holding them hostage in the mirror. "Yes, I guess it really is our last night together, isn't it?" he murmured huskily.

"All of our married life we've done nothing but fight," she whispered brokenly. "Let's try to end our marriage on a more peaceful note. There's nothing we haven't called each other, yelled at each other, or accused each other of. So, for tonight, can't we just be friends?"

He lowered his head and touched his mouth to the dark spot on her shoulder. His voice sounded strained and filled

137

with emotion as he placed soft kisses against the flowery fragrance of her skin. "Oh, Keely, darling. I wish things could be different for us."

His nimble fingers reached for the towel draped around her willowy curves and tugged at it impatiently. His eyes darkened passionately as their gazes met in the mirror for a second time, and he lazily explored the shapely beauty of her naked body.

"You're so beautiful," he marveled, his voice breaking with huskiness. "So very, very beautiful."

Her heart did a double somersault as she turned in his arms to face him. A sense of strength came to her and her despair lessened as she touched her lips sweetly to his.

"Isn't there anything I can do or say that would make you take me back?" he pleaded helplessly, his mouth trembling beneath the pressure of hers. "*Why* can't we be together again!"

"But we could be, Tyler, darling, if you would only listen to reason," she encouraged earnestly, "if you would only give up Sheila and let *me* love you again."

"Oh, darling, Sheila has never meant anything to me. It's always been you, Keely, only you." She could feel the heady sensation of his lips against her neck, and she pressed closer to his intoxicatingly masculine presence. "Just tell me what I have to do to win you back. I'll do anything," he cried urgently. "Anything!"

"You mean you'd be willing to give up Sheila . . . Sheila, who has such lovely, sexy, shiny hair." Her breath was coming in short gasps now as his hands slid down her body stroking her stomach sensuously.

"Oh, you silly, lovable, foolish darling. Next to your beautiful hair, Sheila's looks like a cheap wig. Is that the only thing that's keeping us apart? If so, I'll gladly give up Sheila," he vowed hotly against her neck.

"Well," Keely said surging even closer, her hands caressing him suggestively. "If you'll promise to give up

Sheila, never leave the toilet seat up again, and *never, ever,* buy sixteen cans of bug spray . . ."

"I promise, I promise . . ." he promised.

"Keely . . . are you asleep?" Tyler knelt down beside his wife and shook her on the shoulder gently. "I'm through in the bathroom now."

Keely's eyes flew open, and she experienced a sharp pang of disappointment. It had only been a foolish dream!

"Oh," she mumbled, a bit disoriented. "I must have dozed off. Can I have the bathroom now?"

"Yes, but you're going to have to hurry. We're going to be late." He walked over and sat down on the sofa, reaching for the evening paper.

For a moment she couldn't make her legs move, and she sat staring at him, remembering how tender and wonderful he had been in her dream. She could almost feel the way his lips had come down to smother hers. . . .

"What's the matter?" Tyler cast a glance over in her direction.

"What . . . ?" Keely jerked back to the present.

"I said, what's the matter? Why are you looking at me that way?"

"Oh, I was just thinking," she said, sighing wistfully, then forcing herself to rise from the floor. "I'll hurry."

"Don't break your neck," he said, shaking out the sports section. His eyes noted her disreputable and exhausted condition. "A few more minutes one way or the other isn't going to make any difference." His attitude had changed from brusque to cordial in the blink of an eye.

It did take much longer than Keely planned, so it was well past the time they should have been at the restaurant when they finally arrived.

"We had almost given up on you two," Chris remarked as they were seated at a table next to a window that boasted a spectacular view of the mountains. "Did you try to get your Blazer out of hock before you came over?"

"No, I called the police about it while Keely was in the shower and told them I'd be down to pick it up in the morning," Tyler replied, perusing the menu carefully.

"Has he cooled down any?" Chris teased, whispering conspiratorially into Keely's ear. He was loving every minute of their dilemma.

"He has cooled way down," she nodded solemnly, recalling the stony silence that had accompanied them in the car.

"If you don't mind, I'd rather not get into this discussion again," Tyler advised his partner as he tossed his menu back down on the table. "You look nice tonight, Pam."

"Thank you. I wondered if anyone was going to notice I was here," Chris's wife said, grinning pertly.

"I'm sorry. How are you, Pam?" Keely said, remembering her manners.

"Perfect. Did Tyler tell you about the big deal they closed today?" She looked at her husband proudly. "I think we are now married to two construction tycoons."

"No, he didn't mention anything," Keely replied as she picked up her water glass and took a sip.

"We haven't even had time to discuss my trip since I got home," Tyler offered as a curt excuse. "Chris and I sewed up a pretty hefty contract this afternoon."

"Hefty!" Pam exclaimed. "I would say that's an understatement if I ever heard one!"

Tyler smiled at Pam, his eyes sparkling mischievously. "It *was* a bit more than hefty, wasn't it?"

"A bit. Oh, by the way, not to change the subject, but I was thinking about buying Chris and me a waterbed," she said, grinning embarrassedly, "and I was wondering how you liked yours. You did go ahead and buy one last week, didn't you?"

Tyler glanced at Keely and looked a bit disconcerted. "Yes, I bought one a few days ago." Keely slowly lowered her water glass and stared at him silently.

140

"Well, is it worth the money?" Pam asked.

"Sure, it's very comfortable," Tyler said, looking around uneasily for their waitress. "What do you have to do to get some service around here," he grumbled.

"I've heard they were," Pam chattered on. "I found a lovely one this afternoon, and since you men have made all of us rich, I think I'll go back in the morning and buy it."

"Gee, Tyler, I didn't know your waterbed was brand new," Keely said in mock enthusiasm. "I was under the impression you had slept on it for a while." No wonder he had told her he had never made love in a waterbed! The yo-yo hadn't had it long enough to try it out!

"I don't believe I mentioned how long I had had it," he answered casually, "and I don't believe you asked." He smiled at her solicitously.

The waitress came over and took their orders as Keely seethed inwardly. She had known it had been too good to be true! Tyler Jerico was a hot-blooded . . . barbarian! What a fool she had been to hope he hadn't brought other women onto his . . . his . . . loveboat!

The other three occupants of the table made small talk as Keely sat quietly harboring ill thoughts against her estranged husband. She simply had to hold her temper until she left tomorrow. She was so close to proving that she had not been the instigator of all their problems, and she musn't let his lying ways keep her from that goal. One more night. In fact, she glanced down at her watch, if a person wanted to get technical, she only had a little over three hours to go. Three hours! She could make it! She felt absolutely positive that she could.

When their steaks arrived, she dug into hers with gusto. In a way, it reminded her of the way a condemned man ate his last meal, but she was determined to enjoy one decent meal before she went back home. She had just taken a bite of the juicy steak when she noticed Tyler pick up the catsup bottle and plunk a glob of it on his steak.

He couldn't have missed the sigh of disgust coming from her corner of the table.

"Something wrong, Mrs. Jerico?" he asked, cocking one eyebrow.

"Not a thing," Keely said, averting her attention to her steak once more. "If you want to persist in ruining a good steak with all that catsup, be my guest." She stuck a piece of the tasty morsel in her mouth and chewed contentedly.

Tyler looked down at the mound of catsup lying on his steak, then turned belligerent eyes toward her. "I always eat my steak with catsup on it. What's wrong with that?"

"Not a thing."

The four continued eating in silence, enjoying their delicious fare. As the waitress brought their coffee, she set the creamer on the table and left. Tyler reached over and picked up the container and dumped half of it into his coffee. Keely watched with mocking eyes, eating her salad quietly. Tyler glanced back up and saw her taunting look. "What now?"

"Did I say anything?" she asked, reaching for a hot roll and buttering it liberally.

"Have some sour cream," Chris offered hurriedly, passing the condiment tray to her. "Try some of those bacon bits too. They're great." Keely spooned out the velvety white sauce on her potato and passed the tray to her right.

Tyler took the dish and sat it down next to his plate. Before he touched the spoon to the sour cream, he looked at Keely hostilely. "Do you mind?"

Keely shrugged her shoulders and went on eating. If he wanted to pick a fight, he was out of luck. She only had three hours to go, and she wasn't about to blow it at this late date.

"Oh, look, there's Sheila," Pam said brightly. She stood up and motioned for Sheila to join them. "I asked her to join this little celebration. After all, she's part of JeriMor Construction Company."

142

Keely felt the piece of meat she had just put in her mouth lodge in her throat. Sheila!

"Hi," Sheila bubbled as she approached the table and took a chair next to Tyler. "I didn't know if you would be through eating yet or not."

"Have you had your dinner?" Tyler asked, helping her out of her coat politely.

"I had a carton of yogurt," she said, smiling. "Have to watch the calories, you know."

Keely's eyes dropped to her plate guiltily, a wave of nausea sweeping over her at the sight of all that sour cream, and hot rolls laden with butter glaring back at her. She glanced back up and noticed how perfect Sheila's hair was again. Doesn't that girl *ever* have a hair out of place? she thought angrily.

"I'll just keep all of you company while you finish," Sheila said. She reached over and plucked Tyler's fork out of his hand and stole a bite of his baked potato. "Heavenly!" she sighed, rolling her baby blue eyes in ecstasy.

Keely stifled the urge to destroy her perfect face. *And* perfect hair. *And* perfect figure. She went back to her perfectly awful meal, trying to ignore Sheila and Tyler's amiable clucking over each other.

When the meal was finally over, Keely excused herself and went to the powder room, desperately needing to escape. She berated herself for ever coming tonight. Of course she hadn't known that Sheila would be here or she would have put her foot down and refused Tyler's demand that she come. This was, no doubt, a last-ditch effort on his part to win the bet. If he could flaunt his mistress in his wife's face, he would naturally think that would upset her enough to make her blow her stack. But he was wrong. Dead wrong! A tiny voice rose up in her mind, taunting softly, *Keely Jerico, what makes you so sure that Tyler and Sheila are involved in any way other than business? You certainly have never seen one thing to indicate any different. Tyler has never mentioned the woman's name other than in passing. Yes,* she argued back, *but he's certainly never denied that there was anything between them. That's true,* said the little voice, *but surely if they were in love, there would be more evidence than that to convict them,* the small voice persisted. *Aren't you jumping to conclusions? Butt out!* Keely thought irritably, slamming her purse down on the bathroom vanity. *Who asked you, anyway? If I know Tyler Jerico, he's involved with her!*

It was a long time before Keely could make herself go back out to the table and face the rest of the evening. She had decided to plead a headache and take a cab home as soon as possible. There was absolutely no way she was going to hang around and watch Tyler drool over Sheila all evening.

"Here she is," Pam called as Keely walked back to the table. "We were about ready to send someone after you. Are you all right?"

"I'm fine. I just have a slight headache," Keely said, sitting back down at the table.

"You really should have stopped by the hospital and had someone check you over," Chris chastised her in a fatherly tone. "You could be hurt and not realize it."

"No, really, I'm fine. Just a bit sore," Keely said, smiling at him, "but thank you for your concern."

"She isn't hurt," Tyler said curtly. "If I had thought for one minute she was, I would have taken her to the hospital myself."

"Hey, listen to that music," Sheila said dreamily. "Let's dance, Tyler."

Tyler glanced over at Keely, then stood up abruptly. "That sounds like a good idea, Sheila. You'll excuse us?"

"I'll definitely excuse you," Chris said, rising to his feet simultaneously with them. "I'm going to have to go to the powder room," he trilled in a feminine voice.

Pam laughed and shooed him away with her hand absently. "I don't know how I put up with that man," she told Keely happily. Keely could tell it was no real imposition for Pam. She apparently loved her husband very dearly. "Things aren't going so smoothly, huh?" Pam had an uncanny knack for reading Keely's mind.

"No, I'll be going home in the morning."

"Neither one of you has lost the bet yet?"

"No, we'll just split up the property as originally planned." Keely's eyes closely followed the couple dancing on the deserted dance floor.

"You're still very much in love with him, aren't you?" Pam asked in a soft voice.

"Yes, very much." Keely saw no reason to lie to Pam. She was in love with Tyler. She would always be in love with Tyler.

"It's such a shame you two can't work things out. I happen to think he still loves you too."

Keely let out a small ironic laugh. "I'm afraid not."

"Are you sure?" Pam's eyes held tender compassion for the woman sitting so morosely in front of her.

"Does that look like he's in love with me?" Keely motioned with a gaze toward the dance floor at the couple dancing closely to a slow waltz.

Pam's eyes followed Keely's gesture. "What? You mean Tyler and Sheila?"

"Yes." Keely fingered the corner of the tablecloth nervously. "Obviously he has found someone else."

"Tyler and Sheila?" Pam asked again disbelievingly. "Well, this is certainly news to me!"

Keely glanced up quickly at Pam. "You mean . . . you didn't know?"

"No." Pam's eyes were round as saucers. "Did *he* tell you that?"

"No, not in so many words, but I have eyes . . . and ears."

Pam shook her head, trying to digest this startling piece of information. "Well, boy, they sure have kept it a secret if they're messing around with each other," she said, still unconvinced. Her eyes focused back on the dance floor. "Tyler and Sheila?"

"You mean he hasn't . . . dated a lot since we separated?" Keely felt a small surge of hope spring alive.

Pam answered, "I wouldn't know about that, Keely. Tyler has never discussed his personal life with me, but Chris would surely have mentioned him dating someone. On the contrary, Chris has always said that Tyler should get out more often and try to forget . . . the past." Pam reached over and took her hand. "I do know that he's been awfully depressed and lonely since he came out here six months ago. You know, we tend to think that men can go through a divorce and never be hurt, but that's not true. That's not true at all. They hurt as badly as we women do, only sometimes I think it's harder on them. They don't break down and cry. At least we can bawl our heads off to another woman and feel a little better, but a man doesn't think he has that privilege."

"Oh, Pam, I've cried so many times I can't even count them any longer, and I don't remember ever feeling better. How long will the pain and hurt go on?"

"I don't know. Forever, if you really love him," she sighed softly.

"Then I'm sentenced to life in prison," Keely said, reaching for her napkin to wipe away rising tears, "because I do."

"I really can't help but feel you're wrong about Tyler and Sheila," Pam tried to console her. "Sheila is Chris's sister, and he works with Tyler every day. Don't you think he would notice something that obvious?"

"Maybe Tyler wants to keep it quiet until the divorce is final," Keely said as she fought the tears uselessly. "He might think I'd put a kink in his plans."

The sound of Sheila's bubbly laughter interrupted their conversation. Keely looked toward the dance floor, and her heart thudded painfully in her chest. "Oh, Tyler, you are an absolute doll," Sheila was saying. She threw her arms around his neck and kissed him breathlessly. "I love you!"

Keely caught the last words, "I love you," before she reached blindly for her purse and sprang to her feet.

"Keely." Pam reached out to grab for her, but it was too late. She was already running out the front door before Pam could dislodge herself from the entanglement of the chairs and come after her.

Keely hailed a cab and stumbled into the back seat, tears clouding her vision as she stammered out the address of the apartment. How could he! How could he let Sheila kiss him in front of Chris and Pam. It was so degrading, so demeaning, to think that he would be so callous as to hurt her this way in public. What kind of a heartless man was he? Although he had made it clear to her that the marriage was over, did he have to tell the whole world with her sitting there?

When Keely reached the apartment, she let herself in with the extra key Tyler had given her and slammed the door loudly. He couldn't hear it, but it made her feel better. For the next thirty minutes she paced the floor like a caged animal, calling him everything vile and demeaning she could conjure in her mind. She alternated between pain and anger, tears and defiance. How could she have ever thought she loved this man? Surely there was more to life than constantly battling someone who obviously cared so little for her.

Finally, with a sense of utter desolation, she sank down next to the living room couch and bawled. He had won. She knew that as soon as he walked through that door she would scream at him everything she had been biting back all week long. She would lose everything, but she was powerless to stop herself. He had known all along she would never make it. He was so smug, so arrogant, so very sure that he would be the victor. Keely sat up and wiped her eyes. No! She glanced at her watch and saw that she had only fifteen minutes to go. No! He would *not* be the victor! All of a sudden she started laughing. She was going to make it after all! Only fifteen minutes to go, and Tyler wasn't even home yet! No doubt he had taken Sheila home and decided to stay for a while. Keely picked up a pillow and flung it across the room angrily. She could wring his neck! If he couldn't wait one more day until his wife left town to resume his rakish ways . . .

The sound of the key in the front door brought her back to the present. Tyler! She ran across the room and picked up the discarded pillow and placed it back neatly on the sofa. There would be no sign of any kind of a temper tantrum. She glanced back down at her watch. Twelve minutes. Only twelve lousy minutes to go. When he came in, she would act cool, calm, and collected. She would show him that his outlandish, childish behavior at the restaurant had gone unnoticed by her. If he bothered to inquire about why she had left the restaurant in such a hurry, she would coolly inform him there had been an old movie coming on she had wanted to see. Then she would bid him good night in a polite tone, and make her bed on the couch. Tomorrow morning, after a nice breakfast, he would take her to the plane; they would say good-bye in a reasonable, adult tone, possibly even shake hands. Then she would go home and quietly have a nervous breakdown! Now all she had to do was get through the next twelve minutes tranquilly, and that wouldn't be any problem at all at the moment. She felt very composed.

"Why in hell did you leave the restaurant like a damn scalded cat!" Tyler burst through the door, his face an angry mask. "I've spent the last half hour trying to fight my way across town in all that traffic. I didn't know if you were sick or—"

"If I was sick!" Keely exploded. "If I was sick! You have gone too far this time, Tyler Jerico." She started advancing on him with a dangerous stalking motion, her blue eyes shooting bolts of fire. "You bring your little girl friend to the restaurant and drag her out on the dance

148

floor, holding her tighter than you *ever* held me in your entire life, then let her throw her arms around you and kiss you in front of all those people while your wife's left sitting at the table, looking like an utter fool!"

Tyler began backing up slowly. "Now, Keely, you misunderstood what you saw—"

"Don't you *dare* try to tell me I didn't see Sheila kissing you," she said with a menacing snarl, "or that I didn't hear her say to you, I love you! Are you going to stand there and try to tell me I didn't hear that!" she demanded hotly.

"Now, honey, wait a—" Tyler was running out of backing room fast. "You didn't see what you thought you saw."

"Oh, really, then exactly *what* did I see, Tyler?"

Tyler's back had reached the wall. He reached out and tried to take her in his arms. "Keely, sweetheart, now think about what you're about to do. You're about to lose everything you have by getting all upset over some minor little incident."

"Minor incident!"

"Keely!" Tyler's voice was stern now as he straightened up bravely and faced his irate wife. "You put that ashtray down this min—" The words were never completed, with Tyler breaking away from the wall and starting across the room in a dead run. A heavy object came sailing by him, hitting the wall and shattering into a million pieces. "Now, hold on, Keely!" he thundered.

As Keely grabbed for the lamp on the end table, her eyes caught the clock on the fireplace mantel. It was still five minutes until midnight. Hell's bells! She was bankrupt!

149

CHAPTER NINE

"Keely, I'm warning you! I will not overlook this rampage! You better stop and think what you're—" Another flying missile came zooming by his head. "That does it!" he stormed, trying to dodge a vase that whizzed perilously close. "The bet's over, and *you* lost!" He shouted the last line in an almost gleeful tone of voice as he ducked again rapidly.

"I know I've lost!" she raged, picking up one of his bowling trophies off the mantel and hurling it in his direction. "I lost the day I married you. You never wanted a wife, Tyler Jerico. You wanted a . . . a sparring partner!" A second trophy shot by his cringing form.

"This is ridiculous, Keely; I've never seen you act so—" Two more trophies were lobbed toward him angrily. He ducked swiftly, then straightened up and jammed his fists on his hips furiously. "Hell, Keely! That was the first-place trophy I won for catching the biggest bass in our club last year. Look what you've done to it! You broke the damn fish off the cup!"

"I couldn't care less about your stupid trophies—all I want is for you to sign those divorce papers, then take me to the airport!" she raved. "When I leave here, I never want to see you again!" She snatched up his briefcase lying on the table and propelled it at him. "Sign them this minute!" she screeched.

"I am not signing anything until you stop this juvenile bombardment of me and sit down and try to talk this over sensibly!" Tyler shouted as he tried to retrieve the papers fluttering around the room wildly. "Just please try to calm down before the neighbors call the police!" he pleaded irritably.

She looked around for something else to lay her hands on. The very nerve of that guy suggesting that *she* was being unreasonable after what he had just pulled on her at the restaurant! "Juvenile, huh? You haven't seen anything yet!"

"If you don't stop now, I'm going to pick you up and paddle your bottom like I would an unruly child. You are completely out of control. Now, damn it, Keely, I said knock it off!" He swerved to miss the paperweight she chunked at his head. "Just tell me what you're so upset about!"

"What I'm upset about! Are you nuts, Tyler! You know perfectly well what I'm so upset over. You deliberately set it up, didn't you! You wanted to make sure I would lose the bet!"

"If you're talking about that silly little kiss . . ."

"You knew all along that you could get me to lose my temper, didn't you? Then, when I *didn't* lose it, you panicked and took drastic measures, getting Pam to ask Sheila to come to the restaurant tonight and stage her 'silly little kiss'!"

"That's not true, Keely. I did *not* know that Sheila was coming to the restaurant tonight, and I certainly didn't stage that kiss to make you lose the bet." He took a step across the room toward her, his gray eyes pleading. "Just put that candy dish down, sweetheart, and let's talk this thing over calmly."

He swerved abruptly as the dish burst into fragments

151

against the wall behind his head. When he straightened this time, his eyes were cold slits of fury. "Now, I have *had* it with you, lady! You are going to force me into doing something you're not going to like!"

"You stay away from me, you . . . you . . ." Keely's face went blank. She couldn't think of one single thing to call him that she hadn't already called him before.

"What's the matter, can't you think of a word bad enough?" he taunted as he inched closer to her. "Well, let me help you. How about pervert, womanizer, cradle robber. After all, Sheila's only eighteen or nineteen, and I'm nearly thirty-six."

"If the shoe fits . . ." Keely met his arrogant stare angrily.

With stalking steps he drew closer, a steely look of determination in his eyes now. "All right, Keely, if you persist in your little temper tantrum, then you're going to force me to control you the only way I know how," he told her grimly.

Keely started backing away from him warily, her blood pounding. "You wouldn't dare," she gasped with indignation. "What's the matter, Tyler, isn't one woman enough for you? Do you actually think that you're going to come in here after being with Sheila and *force* me to make love with you. You're crazy!" she stated emphatically.

"I have *never* forced you to make love," he stated with assurance as he inched closer, "and I have *not* come from 'being' with Sheila."

"You stay away from me," she threatened. "If you touch me, I'll scream."

"Scream away," he said, undaunted in his pursuit. "I had the strong impression that's what you've been doing for the last ten minutes anyway. Do you honestly think one more screech out of you is going to bother me?"

Whirling around, Keely started running toward the bedroom, with Tyler following in hot pursuit. "Oh, no, you don't; we're going to get a few things straight between

152

us, Keely Jerico, whether you like it or not." Tyler made a running tackle at her scurrying form, and they both landed with a jarring thud in front of the fireplace.

Keely reached out to slap his face, and one large hand grabbed both of her small ones and pinned them to her side easily. "We're not going to have any scratching, biting, spittin', or hittin' below the belt," he said, laying down the rules, breathing heavily. "This is going to be a nice, clean fight."

"Get off me, you idiot! You're pulverizing me!" Keely squirmed angrily beneath his crushing weight.

"I've never heard you complain before," he grunted, rolling off the top of her, but still keeping her firmly pinned against his solid frame. "Lie still, or I'm going to nail you to the floor," he warned her, trying to still her thrashing feet. "You are the hardest damn woman to carry on a conversation with that I've ever met!"

"I do not wish to converse with you ever again," she said in haughty manner. "Can't you take a hint!"

"Well, I wish to converse with you, so just pipe down for five minutes and let me have my say!"

"You can say all you want. I'm not listening. The only thing I want to hear is the sound of your pen scratching across the bottom of those divorce papers. When that's completed, wake me." Keely closed her eyes tightly. At the moment, she wished she were carrying another two hundred pounds on her slender frame. Then they would see who pinned whom to the floor!

"The first thing we're going to get cleared up is this damn foolishness about Sheila," he said, ignoring her resistance. "I realize that I should have put a stop to your wild imaginings from the beginning, but I suppose I rather liked the feeling of you being the jealous one for a change, and not me."

Keely's eyes flew back open. "What are you talking about!"

"I'm talking about the fact that there is absolutely nothing going on between Sheila Morgan and myself. Good Lord, Keely, she's a little young for me to be messin' around with. And even if she was older, I'm not interested in finding another woman. I can't even handle the one I have—why would I want to take on another headache!"

"Why did she kiss you?" Keely didn't want to listen to him, but she found herself responding unwillingly to his words. His familiar smell, the intimate way his thighs kept hers pinned to the floor, caused her stomach to flutter nervously. Being this close to him brought back too many old memories. Memories of happier times between them. Times when their hands had been occupied with each other's bodies in a more pleasant, happier way.

Tyler's voice softened somewhat as he lay his head down next to hers and sighed defeatedly. "I didn't want to tell you this, but after I saw how upset you became at the restaurant, I realized that what I had done was pretty rotten. Believe me, I know the pain of jealousy, Keely. I'm well aware you don't love me anymore, but it would still have to hurt to see your husband make a pass at another woman. Sheila is a giggly eighteen-year-old, and I know how she reacts to certain situations. She's always been an affectionate girl. So, when I told her she could take a few extra days off over the weekend to go on a ski trip with her boyfriend, I knew exactly what her reaction would be. I did stage that silly little kissing act for your benefit, but not beforehand. It was a spur-of-the-moment idea. A stupid one, I admit, but, at the time, it seemed the thing to do."

"Do you mean to tell me you let me labor under the impression that you and Sheila . . . well, that is downright disgusting! How could you lie to me like that!"

"I didn't lie to you," he said in a defensive voice. "I just didn't tell you any different when you kept bringing her name up."

"You knew all along that I thought that you and she . . ."

"Yes," he said quietly. "I knew what you thought. But I also knew you never played it straight with me about Craig." He propped himself up on his elbow and looked at her in the flickering flames of the fireplace. "If you're honest, Keely, you'll admit you used your womanly wiles on your own husband. Oh, I know you always said there was nothing going on between you and Craig, but you still could look at me with that little mysterious smile and leave me wondering."

Keely lowered her eyes from his serious gaze. A strong wave of guilt washed over her. What he said was true. She had always said she was innocent, but she was woman enough to make him stew just a bit. "I'm sorry," she said, meeting his eyes once again. "You're right. I did do that. Not because I wanted to make you jealous, but I guess every woman has that little secret longing to see her husband go to pieces at the thought of losing her. You would have never lost me, Tyler, not to another man. Not at that time."

Tyler's voice turned husky as he reached out and touched the creamy perfection of her soft skin. "Are you telling me you're in love with another man?"

She had lost the bet, she had lost her husband, she had lost everything but her pride. She would not lose that now! "Yes," she whispered gently. "I'm in love with a man."

"Craig?" he asked miserably.

"No, not Craig. The man I'm in love with is married. His divorce will be final around the time mine is," she added quickly. She bit back the tears at the look of utter desolation that overcame his features.

"Well, at least we're finally able to tell each other the truth," he sighed. "Is he going to marry you when the divorce is final?"

"No, he told me he has no plans of remarrying in the near future." Why was she doing this to him? Why didn't she scream out the fact that she was talking about him. Not some strange man. But their marriage was over, and she would not crawl away on her hands and knees in defeat. She would leave this marriage with her head held high, even though it might very well destroy her.

Tyler's eyes blazed resentfully for a brief moment. "Who is the bum?"

"It doesn't matter who the 'bum' is," she said tightly. "What matters is that I've finally said what you've been wanting me to say ever since we got married."

"Now, what are *you* talking about?"

"It's true, Tyler; you even said so yourself. From the very first, you've been searching for an opportunity to, I believe your exact words were, 'get the pain and hurt over with.' You have always been so sure that I was going to walk out on you, just like every other person in your life had. I think that's why you continually quarreled over trivial things, why you always accuse me of being unfaithful. I know that I was at fault many times, also, but how would you have felt if I had accused you of seeing other women?"

"You're right." Tyler released her hands and brought one of his arms up to cover his eyes. "You're absolutely right. But at that time I didn't see that, Keely. So help me God."

"And you do now?" Her pulse fluttered. Could he finally admit the truth?

"I've been seeing a doctor for the last few months. He's helped me to see a lot of things that I could never see before." Tyler's voice held no emotion now, only tired resignation.

"You've been seeing a psychologist?" Keely asked in quiet surprise.

"There's nothing wrong with that," Tyler said defensively. "Actually he's a marriage counselor too."

"Well, no, I didn't mean there was anything wrong in that, I'm just a little surprised, that's all." It was so unusual for Tyler to ask for help. He had always been so hellbent on doing things his way.

156

"I had a lot of things gnawing at me, things that I didn't understand. I finally came to the decision that I couldn't handle my feelings alone, so I made an appointment with Dr. Jacobs. I've never regretted it. There's nothing unmanly about that," he reminded her again in a small voice.

"No, I think that's very manly," she answered tenderly. "I know how hard that must have been for you."

"It wasn't hard when I stopped to think back on my life, and what a damn mess I had made of our marriage."

"It takes two to wreck a marriage," she said kindly, trying to ease his pain. "We should both have gone to a marriage counselor when things started to get out of hand."

"I probably wouldn't have gone then," Tyler said thoughtfully. "I can get pretty bullheaded sometimes."

"No kidding." Keely had to laugh.

"And," Tyler said, rolling back over to face her, "so can you."

Keely smiled at him knowingly and said, "And, so can I."

"I hope this clown that you're in love with knows what he's getting," he said in a low and purposely seductive voice. His eyes glowed with a curious deep longing as he gazed at her in the flickering firelight.

"If you dare tell him, I'll wring your neck," she teased lightly.

"I hope to hell I never have to meet him," he said, his voice dropping huskily.

The sound of the fire crackling in the grate filled the sudden silence of the room. Keely didn't know what to say to him. Now wasn't the time to tell him of her spontaneous fib. If she were wise, *never* would be the appropriate time to mention it.

"If the guy isn't interested in marriage, what's the future in seeing him?" Tyler asked, trying to keep his voice as casual as possible.

"I don't want a future with him," Keely said uncom-

157

fortably. His eyes seemed to penetrate her very soul. "I've decided never to marry again. I'm just going to live it up," she babbled. "When I get back home, I'm going to start going to all the singles bars with my friends."

Tyler grunted distastefully.

"No, I really am," she insisted. "I haven't in the past because they always left for the bars so early I didn't have time to go with them."

"Left early?"

"Yes," she sighed resignedly. "Their theory is, the men with the gold chains around their neck go fast."

"Hell, Keely! You're not serious!" Tyler said disgustedly.

"Oh, yes, I am. I'm going to turn wilder than a March hare," she said in a solemn voice.

Tyler's deep laughter rumbled across the room. "Tell me another one! It took you three months to let me see you in the shower when we first married. Are you trying to tell me you've become a . . . uh—"

"No! Not one of those," she said primly. "I'll be selective." She grinned at him impishly.

"A selective March hare. Hmmm . . . sounds interesting." Again the mischievous look came into his eyes. "The way we're lying here in front of the fire, does that remind you of anything?"

"No," Keely said abruptly. She knew exactly what it reminded him of. Her mind hadn't been off the old memories since he had first landed on her on the floor.

"Oh, now, come on," he persisted. "Think hard. You don't remember all the times we used to make love in front of *our* fireplace?"

Keely moved around uneasily. "Tyler, what difference does it make now? You've won the bet, and tomorrow I go home and our marriage is over. I don't want to talk about . . . old times."

He bent his head slightly forward and grinned at her

158

boyishly. "I just thought since you were going to be a selective March hare you might just like to select me for one night. I mean, this is going to be our last night together," he reasoned, "and you're a lovely, desirable woman, and I'm a handsome, virile man who can always go put on a gold chain." His voice dropped to a deep base tone as he continued. "And we *are* still married." He wiggled his eyebrows at her.

"Tyler, stop teasing," Keely whispered brokenly. She didn't even want to joke about this touchy subject, not when every cell of her being cried out for him.

"Who in hell's teasing?" he said seriously, his eyes turning to a dark smoky gray. "I want to make love to you." His hand reached out to touch her face gently. "I think you want me to make love to you, too, my beautiful wife. I can see it written in those enchanting eyes of yours."

"No, Tyler." Keely blinked back the tears.

"Don't tell me no. You don't mean a word of it." His lips touched hers with delicious enticement. "Do you?"

"Yes, I do," she murmured as her tongue automatically met with his. They teased each other for a moment, then he nipped at her lips with his even white teeth.

"Is the answer still no?" he asked again, pulling her tightly against him to let her feel the full measure of his desire for her.

"Yes . . . no . . . maybe," she said, beginning to crumble.

"Is that a multiple-choice question?" He brushed his mouth against her ear. "If it is, I choose maybe."

"You *are* incorrigible." She smiled, kissing the tip of his nose.

"I *am* in pain," he corrected her, grinning at her devilishly. "And," he continued in a persuasive tone, "it's a shame to let that gorgeous waterbed go untouched. I bought it for you, you know."

"For me! How did you know that I would share it with you . . . you . . ."

159

Tyler smiled down upon her radiant loveliness. "I know you, hot stuff."

"Am I that transparent?" She blushed.

"Don't let me mislead you, I love it. Now, back to the original question." His mouth moved over hers again in a tantalizing resumption of his seduction.

She knew she would hate herself later. She knew that it was wrong to be so weak; but she knew that she still desperately loved the man who lay beside her. So she let that thought override all others.

Her answer was to bring his mouth down to meet hers in a kiss as tender and light as a summer breeze.

"I hope that means yes," he whispered against her lips softly.

"I mean . . . yes," she said breathlessly. "Yes, yes, yes."

She succumbed to the forceful domination of his lips willingly, a moan of ecstasy slipping through her throat. His hand trembled as he reached down to unbutton her blouse, and he laughed nervously as he broke the kiss for a brief second. "This is crazy; I feel like a teenager on his first try."

Molten tenderness rose within her as she reached up and slowly began to undress him, pausing between each button to stroke the dark hair on his chest she had longed for so long to bury her hands in. "Do you want me to take my blouse off?" She made the offer a low, sexy challenge.

"No, I think I can handle it," he said, grinning as the last button came undone. Within moments he had shed all of his clothes and stripped her of hers.

"It's amazing how fast you went from a teenage boy to a grown-up, lustful man," she complimented him teasingly between slow, languid kisses. "However did you manage to get over your shyness that quickly?"

"There's just some March hares that bring out the best in me," he returned proudly as his lips touched first one of her nipples, then the other, tantalizing those buds, which had swelled to their fullest. His hands and mouth began a slow, arousing exploration of her soft flesh. Her body melted against his, and her hands explored down his thighs, then moved up his taut stomach.

"Did I ever tell you how beautiful I thought you were?" he murmured as his tongue made a path down her ribs to her stomach, "or how I thought your eyes were the color of turquoise in the early morning light?"

"Robin's eggs," she gasped as his hand moved up to grasp hers and guided it gently to himself. "You told me they were the color of robin's eggs one time."

They kissed long and deep, and she felt transformed and on a soft and wispy cloud. Her body seemed to vibrate as her hand ardently caressed him, making him moan with pleasure.

Suddenly he stood up and pulled her to her feet, his eyes devouring the shapely beauty of her naked body. She felt very vulnerable standing before him in the rosy firelight, and she longed to yield to the burning sweetness that seemed a prisoner within her.

"Dance with me," he whispered, reaching out to slowly draw her to him. "Dance with me just one more time. I want to feel you in my arms, touch your skin, smell the wildflowers in your hair." His eyes never left hers as he reached over and quietly switched on the radio. The hushed strains of a love song filtered through the air as he pulled her tightly against his hair-rough chest. It was flesh against flesh, man against woman.

They swayed together gently to the muted tones of the music, exchanging hungry kisses with each other, oblivious to the world and all its riddles. The flames of passion burned bright between them as Tyler whispered in a soft throaty voice the words of "The Rose" in her ear. He kissed the pulsing hollow at the base of her throat as his hands slipped up her arms, bringing her ever tighter against him. Raising his mouth from her dewy skin, he gazed into her passion-laden eyes with smoldering gray pools that were clouded hurtfully with the past. "Did I

161

ever take the time to tell you how much I loved you?" he murmured sorrowfully.

She could only nod back at him wordlessly, touched by the sincerity in his voice.

"I did, Keely. I loved you more than my own life. I just couldn't find a way to tell you as often as I should have."

She buried her face against the corded muscles of his chest, love flowing through her veins like the torrent of water through the floodgates of a dam. "We both should have told each other more often," she acknowledged quietly.

"Don't let that happen between you and the man you love now, Keely. Don't be afraid to let each other know how much you care."

He took her mouth with savage intensity, the passion of his ardor mounting out of control. "I want you, sweetheart, give me one more memory of you to last a lifetime," he whispered, his breath hot against her ear.

Gently she was lifted up in his arms, and he carried her over in front of the fire and laid her down tenderly. His mouth recaptured hers, and she moaned softly as he lowered his large body over hers, his tongue hungrily searching out the moist recesses of her mouth. Waves of ecstasy throbbed through her as they became one, and they started to move leisurely together in a tempo of sweet agony, their bodies in perfect harmony. Her emotions whirled and eddied as they both soared to awesome, shuddering ecstasy, with her knowing that this would be the last time in his arms. The last time she would ever feel his lips on her breasts, his tongue searing its way down the length of her body, his hands grasping her hair and holding on tightly as spasms racked and shuddered through his body, sending them both into a universe of color, light, and music.

Only the sound of their erratic breathing could be heard as Tyler collapsed in exhaustion beside her. His arms kept her safely within the cradle of his chest as they lay quietly for a moment, savoring the languid, melting feeling that had overtaken their bodies. Keely snuggled closer against him, her leg entwining with his hair-bristled leg. Peace and contentment flowed like a gentle mountain stream through her mind. This is what had made all of it worth it. All the fighting, all the hurting, all the accusations—they would always be forgotten when they had come together in the act of love. When they were in each other's arms, the world seemed to disappear, and, with it, all their problems and heartaches. But, sadly, they couldn't spend the rest of their lives in bed together. There was a world outside their bedroom, a world that they couldn't seem to conquer.

With a sigh of contentment Tyler reached over and drew her face around to meet his. His eyes were lazy and sensual in the mellow afterglow of their lovemaking. "It was always good for us, wasn't it? Through it all, this part of our life was close to perfect."

"Yes, this part was perfect," she agreed sleepily, kissing the dimple in his cheek. How she loved the clean, fresh, manly smell he always emitted. A smell of soap, after-shave, and musk. "There were other good things too," she added. "Remember how we used to love to go over to Jaspers and eat those hamburgers with the big onions on them, and have heartburn for hours? Or how we used to love to lie in bed at night and watch those old John Wayne movies together while we munched on popcorn?" she giggled. "Do you know I lost ten pounds the first month we were separated!"

His hand was absently stroking the silken skin of her thigh, still holding her possessively against his naked body. "I beat you, I lost fifteen," he laughed.

"Oh, you! You always could lose weight ten times faster than I could. Remember how we used to go on a diet, and you would have lost all your extra weight in three days, while I was still trying to choke down carrot sticks and celery? Then you would torment me by stopping by Munson's bakery and bringing home a sack full of those yummy caramel rolls that I was crazy over?"

"Yeah," he said, grinning tenderly. "Boy, wouldn't one of those taste good right now?"

"Yes, if we had some, I could put them in the microwave and warm them up. I think I could eat at least five right now."

Tyler rolled over on his back, bringing her with him. They lay in each other's arms, kissing quietly, his hands running over every curve that he had been so familiar with in the past. Time had no meaning for them, only the pleasure of being in each other's arms once more occupied their minds.

"What do you think, pretty lady? Do you think it would be possible to start again?" Tyler whispered between kisses.

"I don't know, Ty." Keely's heart leapt at his words. Would it be possible for them to make a clean start? To rid themselves of their old troubled marriage and work toward a new, happier one? In many ways they had both changed, matured. But they were still so very much alike in other, old, bothersome ways.

"You don't know how many nights I've lain awake thinking about you, sweetheart. Nights I wanted you so bad it was downright torture."

"I know. I've had plenty of nights like those."

"But it always comes back to the same old question. Is it worth all the haggling we go through?"

Keely's eyes shone with love as she gazed down into the somberness of his. "And what do you think?"

"After one of those nights, I used to decide anything was worth having you back again. But, to be honest, Keely, I'm still the same man I always was. Even though I see myself in a clearer light now, there would still be times when we'd argue, when I would go out of my head with jealousy."

"Tyler, *all* married couples have fights. That's just a

164

part of living, and loving. We just shouldn't let ours get out of hand."

"I know, I know," he said, patting her bottom affectionately, "but take, for instance, this man you're . . . in love with . . . If you and I tried to patch things up, I'd hound you to death until I found out his name. Then I would worry constantly, afraid that you were still in . . . love . . . with him." He still found it extremely hard to utter those words, but he knew she had every right to a new life, free from him.

Keely's teeth came down on her bottom lip, and her face grew thoughtful as she mulled his words over in her mind. Heaving a resigned sigh, she took his face in her two hands and said quietly, "There is no other man, Tyler. I was talking about you when I said I loved a married man."

Tyler's eyes flashed relief, then turned aggressive. "Why in hell did you tell me that then!"

"I told you that because . . . because I had lost the bet and I didn't want to lose what little pride I had left. I didn't want you to think that I couldn't live without you," she said defensively.

"Now, that's what I was talking about, Keely," he said, his voice beginning to show signs of exasperation. "*You* were using your womanly wiles again on me to make me jealous. Why do you do that when you know how that hacks me off!"

"I was not using my womanly wiles on you. I told you I did it because I wanted to save face. You've financially sent me to the poorhouse, taken away everything, what did you want me to do, lie down and let you walk on me?" She slid off his chest in a huff.

"Hey, now, wait a minute," Tyler said, reaching for her bare leg, "don't go getting all riled up. I just happen to think that's a dirty trick to pull on me."

"This just goes to show, Tyler, that we are totally unsuited for each other." She stood up and started to put her clothes back on hurriedly. "You will always be a hot-headed . . ."

"Don't start, Keely!" Tyler sat up and jerked his underwear out from under her feet. She nearly tripped and fell on her face as the briefs were pulled out from beneath her.

"Darn it, Tyler! Watch what you're doing," she exploded.

"*You* get out of the middle of my clothes," he said hastily, jerking on his shirt. "And off my back! Everything was going fine until *you* got mad again."

"I'll get off your back, permanently," she said between clenched teeth. Hopping around on one foot, she pulled her slacks back on, giving him a withering stare. "First thing tomorrow morning!"

"Don't they have a plane leaving tonight?"

She ignored his sly insinuation and reached down to pick up her shoes. "And to think, I was actually thinking about giving you another chance a few minutes ago! Well, let me tell you something, *Mister* Jerico, when I leave here in the morning, with the signed divorce papers, you will never lay eyes on me again! Is that clear? Don't you consider calling me, writing a letter, or any other form of communication. Is that clear? You will never see my face again!"

"Promises, promises," he said belligerently as he stood up and slipped his trousers back on.

"*You* are rude and hateful."

"*You* are an idiot."

Keely whirled and marched to the linen closet, muttering vilely under her breath. "*You* are sleeping on the sofa tonight!" she said firmly.

"The hell I am." He crossed his arms and planted his body firmly in her path, blocking her way to the sofa.

Well, it had been worth a try. She thought that if he saw how upset she was, he might not want to push his luck. He would then relent and let her spend her last night here in comfort. So much for that lunacy!

166

Keely dragged down the blankets and sheets and stomped back to the couch. "Sign those divorce papers. I won't be able to rest tonight until I know I'm rid of you!"

"Ha! You're not going to be able to rest tonight, period," he snorted, watching her make up the dreaded couch. "And I'm not signing those damn divorce papers until the morning. I want to call my lawyer and be sure he can get a revision for the terms of the divorce over here first thing tomorrow. Then I'm sticking your fanny on the first thing that heads south, if I have to tie you to a goose!"

"Oh . . . you are despicable! *Mean* and despicable!"

"You betcha! I'm one hundred and eighty-five pounds of creepin' hell." He grinned smugly.

Keely paused and turned around to face him. "Do you really think you're bothering me?"

Tyler studied her face for a moment. "I imagine I'm irritating the devil out of you."

"Well, you're wrong. If you don't mind, I'm very tired and would like to get some sleep. I have a long trip ahead of me in the morning."

Tyler shrugged, then walked toward the bedroom. "Are you planning on fixing breakfast in the morning?"

Keely clenched her teeth. Brother! The nerve of this man, thinking about breakfast at a time like this! "No! I'm not planning on fixing *your* breakfast in the morning!" she said, stressing her point.

Tyler shrugged his broad shoulders once more. "I would have been better off marrying that woman mud wrestler I used to go with. At least *she* would cook for me."

"You're about as funny as an abscessed tooth." She punched her pillow and slapped it down on the couch sharply.

"Now look, damn it!" Tyler strode back over to the sofa angrily. "I thought we were finally getting somewhere a little while ago, Keely. I admit I still feel something for you, and I'm willing to ask you nicely to come back to me,

167

and we'll try again. We'll both go to a marriage counselor and maybe he can help me to learn how to live with your damn stubbornness and explosive temper, but you're going to have to meet me halfway, lady. You're going to have to get that chip off your shoulder, come off your high horse, and help me figure out a way to save this damn marriage." He shook his finger under her nose irritably. "I still love you, damn it, but you're going to have to shape up—or ship out!"

Keely stared at him with her mouth gaping. These were not the tender words of reconciliation she had hoped to hear! "Oh, you devil with a silver tongue," she chided in a sugary voice. "If you think you can sweet-talk me into starting over—"

"Cut the crap. Do you want to try again or not? I'm not asking twice." His face was a stern, cold mask, warning her he would brook no argument from her at the moment.

"No. I do not want to try again." The words hurt, but so had the man hurt her. She would not lower herself to accept such an offer.

"All right. Just remember *you* were the one who said no. Not me." He turned and walked toward the bedroom purposefully. "I'm through trying, Keely. That's my final offer."

I'll remember you, she thought bitterly, wiping at her tears as he left the room. *I'll always remember you, Tyler Jerico!*

And, she thought sadly, she knew she would.

CHAPTER TEN

The quiet rustle of papers sounded ominous, and very lonely to Keely as she swallowed hard and took another sip of her tasteless coffee. Tyler sat at the kitchen table, reading over the divorce settlement one final time. He had been up early this morning, talking on the phone to his lawyer. Within an hour the lawyer had dropped off a revision of the settlement, stating that Keely would willingly transfer all her community property to Tyler, subject to court approval. All that remained was for Tyler to pick up the pen and make the necessary signature that would terminate their relationship.

Tyler turned the pages slowly, his features cold and aloof: Keely avoided any eye contact with him for fear of breaking down in tears. She was determined he would not see her cry again.

With a sigh of defeat he tossed the papers down on the table before him and asked in a tired voice, "Are you sure this is what you want, Keely?"

Keely stirred her coffee, fighting to push her voice past the constricting lump in her throat. "I don't see any other alternative." She forced herself to look at his beloved face now, the lump in her throat growing tighter. "Do you?"

she asked. How she wished he could come up with some magical, wonderful answer that would make them both new people. Two new people who could fall into each other's arms and spend eternity there together.

"No, I don't know any other way." The gray of his eyes was not as bright this morning. The tired lines around them were more pronounced. Keely knew that he hadn't gotten any more sleep the night before than she had. She had heard him restlessly pacing the bedroom floor long into the night. As she had lain awake listening to his muted footsteps, she had marveled at how two people could destroy each other's lives in so short a time. How two people who had loved so deeply could bring such anguish to each other. It all seemed so very unfair.

Tyler's hand reached down for the pen lying on the table and picked it up slowly. For a brief moment their eyes met, and, in that moment, their very souls were laid bare to the other. All the pain, frustrations, and heart-breaking disappointments flooded their gazes as they silently said good-bye to what had once been a fragile and lovely thing between them. Keely's eyes told Tyler all the things she couldn't bring herself to speak out loud, while his eyes told her he loved her, one final time. When Keely became aware her vision of him had faded in the flood of tears that suddenly erupted, she tore her gaze from his and stared blindly into her coffee cup. As determined as she was not to let him see her cry, she couldn't stop the flow of scalding wetness cascading down her cheeks as she heard the scratch of the pen on the despised paper. It was finally going to be over, but that thought held no elation for her. Tyler Jerico would never be hers again. She would never lie in his arms at night, holding him close. She would never hear his laughter ringing out in a room, strong and clear. She would never touch the thickness of his hair, kiss the softness of his lips, feel the hardness of his broad chest, share another Christmas, grow another year older with him, suffer the agonizing joy of bringing his child into the world—all of that was now gone forever.

Tyler laid the pen down and stacked the papers neatly. Avoiding her look, he handed them to her, then stood up brusquely and walked back over to pour himself another cup of coffee. Neither one spoke, and the silence of the room seemed to enclose them in a tortured world of their own. After all the months of shouting and screaming, their marriage had ended with a whimper, and neither one knew anything more to say.

"I guess I should call the airport." Keely managed to stand up without her legs buckling under her. She hesitantly reached down and sadly picked up the papers, sticking them in her purse.

"I've already taken care of all that. But you had better get your things packed. You leave in an hour." Tyler stood at the window, looking out at the bleak, cold day. The first flakes of snow were beginning to swirl in the air. Any other time he would have welcomed a snowfall, but today—today held no beauty for him.

"I'll pack, then call a cab," Keely murmured as she emptied her cup into the sink, then walked toward the door.

"There's no need for that; I'll take you." His voice sounded very deep in the quiet room.

"Thank you, I won't be long." Keely left the kitchen before she broke down completely. Within thirty minutes she was packed, and they were walking out to the Blazer. The cold air whipped around her ears, making her long for the thick mane of hair that used to shield them so warmly.

"It looks like there's a storm moving in," she observed above the whine of the wind.

Tyler made no comment as he got in on the driver's side and started the motor. He had barely spoken a word since she had left the kitchen earlier.

They backed out onto the street. The snowflakes were becoming larger, swirling puffily through the air. Keely watched absently as they melted against the Blazer as fast as they lit.

"I don't like to fly during bad weather," she said, wishing that he would say something to her. "I sometimes get airsick."

"There's a lot of sickness in the world," he said curtly. Well, at least he was going to make it easier on her to leave him.

They drove for another ten minutes before he turned off the highway and headed in what seemed to her a different direction from the airport. Another few minutes passed before he roared into a parking space next to a large building. Keely glanced around, then looked at him blankly. "Where are we?"

"At the bus station."

"Bus station?" Keely's gaze focused on a large Greyhound bus, which a line of passengers was boarding. "Why are we stopping here?"

"This is where you get on the bus to go home, sweetheart."

"But I'm flying home!" she protested.

"Not out of my pocket, you're not. I'm not about to pay for an airplane ticket when I can send you home on a bus." Tyler jerked her suitcase out of the back and slammed the door shut.

"You're kidding! You're going to stick me on a . . . a . . . *bus!*" she fumed.

"That's right," he said in a singsong voice. "Won't that be fun!"

"Why you . . . you . . ." Keely sputtered as she stumbled out of the car. "This is an outrage!"

"You're going to have to start pinching pennies, honey, and you might as well start right now," he stated firmly as he took her hand and practically dragged her up to the ticket counter.

"Tyler, it will take me days to get back home on this bus. How can you do this to me? Look at the weather.

172

What if the bus has a wreck? The roads are going to get slick . . ." Keely's voice trailed off as they reached the ticket booth.

"One way to Dallas." Tyler laid the money down on the counter defiantly.

"Well, I never!" That louse was actually going to send her home on a bus!

"The bus is loading right now, mister," the ticket agent warned him, taking the money and handing Tyler back the ticket. "Ramp four."

Picking her suitcase back up, Tyler grabbed her hand again and pulled her along through the crowd.

"Let go of me," she hissed. "You're making a scene, you . . . you . . . half-wit!"

"I don't want you to miss your bus," he told her hurriedly, shoving through the crowd.

"Oh, don't worry, you're not going to be stuck with me one more day! I'd leave town today if I had to hire a dogsled, you . . . you . . . imbecile!"

"I'm really going to miss all those sweet little nothings you hurl at me all day, honey. Do you want me to kiss you good-bye?" They had reached the bus, and Tyler handed the porter her bag and turned to face her smilingly.

"I want you to take a flying leap!" Keely said hotly as she brushed past him and stomped up the bus steps.

"Take good care of her, driver. Contrary to appearances, she is a woman. Her hair is just growing out from the brain surgery she had a few weeks ago." Tyler saluted her, and the driver then stepped back as the doors on the bus whooshed shut.

Keely made her way back to a window seat and sat down angrily. This divorce was the best thing that could ever happen to her! Tyler Jerico was a clod of the highest caliber!

She peered out the window of the bus, trying to get one final look at her boorish, highly annoying, but damned lovable adversary. She couldn't deny herself one final glimpse of the man she loved. The object of her affections was leaning insolently against the building, his arms crossed in Indian fashion, staring moodily at the section of the bus she was seated in. The powerful sound of the motor being revved up filled the snow-clouded air as Keely leaned close to the window. The white flakes covered Tyler's hair as he straightened up slowly, a painful look stealing across his handsome features as he realized the bus was starting to pull away. He moved away from the building and ran slowly alongside the window. As their eyes met, each knowing it would be for the last time, Keely reached up and spread her palm flat against the window, longing for one final touch of his hand. His large palm came up to press against hers on the other side of the pane, his gray gaze as dark and stormy as the day. The bus pulled away, leaving him standing alone in the whirling, blinding snow. She turned in her seat and watched until he became only a blur, only a memory in her agonized mind.

The next few hours Keely spent staring out into the cold landscape, her mind a numbed and bruised tormentor. She willed herself to ignore the pain, to concentrate on the way the snow hit the panes of glass. Her hand automatically reached up several times during the interminable day and touched the spot he had touched during those poignant moments, and her eyes would fill with tears as her fingers lovingly stroked the glass before she self-consciously let them drop back down to her lap. She had to pull herself together. Start her life anew. There was no reason why she couldn't. She was a very self-assured woman, one who didn't need a man in her life to justify her existence. She didn't need Tyler Jerico; he was like a hot fudge sundae with mounds of whipped cream and nuts. She certainly didn't need it, she just wanted it!

It was very late at night when the bus pulled into her hometown. This had been one of the most miserable days of her life, and she longed for the seclusion of her apartment, where she could shut out the world and cry out at the injustice of love. Love was only for the lucky, the survivors. At the moment she felt she was neither one.

As she unlocked the door to the apartment she had shared with Tyler, she knew that she would have to find another place to live. There were too many old memories lurking in the corners, waiting to grab at her ghoulishly. The small apartment was cold and empty. Her eyes fell on the fireplace, the ashes a mute reminder of how dead her world had become once more. She made her way slowly through the dark rooms, never bothering to switch on a lamp. She wanted to stay in the dark tonight. If she turned on a light, she knew her problems would become unbearable. In the darkness of the room, she could pretend that tomorrow would be a brighter day. Even if she knew better.

When she reached their . . . her . . . bedroom, she slid the coat from her shoulders and let it fall to the floor. With a tired sigh she lay down on the bed and for the first time that day let the tears come as they would. No longer did she try to stop the terrible outpouring of pain that threatened to consume her.

"Well, hell's bells, woman, you're getting me all wet," a deep masculine voice teased gently.

Keely's eyes flew open in fright, and her heart thudded painfully against her ribs. Hesitantly, her hand crept over to the other side of the bed and encountered a firm-muscled thigh. Jerking to an upright position, she leaned down and peered closely at the dark form hopefully. "Tyler?" she whispered unbelievingly.

"You were expecting Tom Selleck, maybe?"

"Tyler?" She couldn't believe her eyes, but he was lying right here next to her, and by the tender way he was speaking to her, she knew he was no longer mad at her.

"I believe you got away at the bus station before I could kiss you good-bye," he said, rolling over to take her in his

175

arms lovingly. "You don't mind if I take care of that little item before we start arguing again."

"Tyler?" She could not get the fact to register, that Tyler, her Tyler, was actually here beside her!

Suddenly the full impact of him being there hit her, and she hurled herself in his arms, no longer caring about her pride. If she had to, she would beg him to reconsider the divorce. It was true, she could live without him, but, oh, she didn't want to. She showered kisses around his lips and along his jawline, babbling almost incoherently, "You're here, you're really here!" Her mouth met his with an explosion of ravishing kisses, her hands gripping the front of his shirt as if he were the only piece of floating debris from a shipwreck.

"Hey, wait a minute," he chuckled intimately between frenzied kisses. "I'm supposed to be doing this . . . Keely!"

She had already unbuttoned his shirt and was now in the process of unzipping his trousers and stripping them off him eagerly.

"I don't know what's come over you, but don't stop now," he moaned as her mouth came back down on his hungrily. His hands reached out to pull her up tightly against his long and tensing length.

"Don't talk, just love me," she managed to murmur between delicious waves of desire as his hands swiftly divested her of her clothes.

"I can do that, sweetheart," he whispered against her lips fervently. "I have always been able to do that." This time he became the aggressor as his hands began an urgent search down her exquisite curves. Within minutes they were lost in a downpour of fiery sensations. She felt her breasts crush against the granite of his chest, and she desperately needed more of him. As his hand tenderly searched her body to caress the softness that would bring her pleasure, she drowned in a whirlpool of love and need. The world had stopped spinning, and, once again, she was in the arms of the man she loved.

"I thought about this moment all day," Tyler confessed as her hands eagerly sought to touch every part of his naked flesh. It felt so right, so perfect, to have his body pressed intimately against hers once more.

His mouth left hers, kissing its way down the silken path of her slender neck. "You feel so good," he murmured just before he reached her breast. Gently he teased a pink crest with his tongue, rousing a melting sweetness within her.

"I still can't believe you're here . . . you're actually here!" Keely whispered in a small voice as his tongue and teeth continued to send her passion racing to a fevered pitch.

"Oh, I'm here, sweetheart," he assured her as his bold maleness met her warm femininity. "I'm here."

"Don't ever leave me again, Ty," she begged as her body surged upward to meet his. As their bodies blended rapturously with each other, Tyler groaned with unrestrained passion, his mouth merging hotly with hers.

Her body was half ice, half flame, as she moaned against his ear, crying out for release. Their pleasure was pure and explosive as he claimed her body as his, soaring higher and higher until the very peak of delight was reached. His mouth covered hers hungrily as their bodies trembled together and he freed her in a showering burst of sensations.

When they were finally able to speak, he buried his face in the sweetness of her hair and murmured softly, "I love you, Keely. There's no way on earth I'm going to let you go. I know I signed those damned divorce papers, but I'll spend every penny I have to fight you on this thing. If you insist on going through with it, then we'll start again with a fresh new marriage. We are meant for each other, and you better get that through your stubborn head!"

"Fight me! Oh, Tyler, I love you. You wouldn't have to fight me on that."

Tyler chuckled. "Well, that will probably be the *only*

thing we won't fight over, but after the bus pulled out of the station this morning, I came to the painful conclusion that I would rather spend one day fighting with you than a lifetime of living in harmony with someone else." His mouth captured hers again, and she drank in the sweetness of his kiss.

"How did you beat me here," she finally managed to ask minutes later, stroking the bare skin of his back and broad shoulders lovingly.

"I had Chris fly me down in the company plane. I knew I would get here hours before you did."

"Hours! You almost beat me by days! Did you know that stupid bus broke down, and we had to transfer to another one? We sat out on that highway for three hours before another one came to pick us up."

"Isn't that a shame!" Tyler offered her a smile of satisfaction.

"You . . ." He covered her mouth with his again in a persuasive kiss.

"Let's avoid the subject of the bus. It was rotten, and I admit it."

They kissed long and leisurely, all subjects of contention forgotten for the moment. Only their hands were busy, loving each other in all the old familiar places.

"Were you really serious about not wanting the divorce?" she whispered much later, after another fiery round of lovemaking had ignited between them.

"Of course, I'm serious," Tyler murmured sleepily. "We can make it together."

"I know we can, Tyler, but I want you to be absolutely sure in your mind that there has never been anything between Craig and me."

"I told you the other day I believed you when you said there wasn't."

Keely gazed at him seriously. "I know what you told me. I want to know if you *really* meant it."

"Do you know how I found out you were at that restaurant the night we split up?" he asked suddenly. His hand gripped hers tightly.

"No, how? I have my suspicions though," she admitted somberly.

"I received a phone call from a man who refused to give his name, telling me my wife was having dinner with her lover."

"Tyler!"

"I went to pieces, Keely. I was ready to kill you and Craig both that night. Now I think I know who made that phone call, and the reason behind it. If you'll forgive me, I'll promise to make 'trust' the first ingredient in our new commitment. I want this marriage to succeed. I love you."

"You know I'll forgive you. I love *you*, Tyler Jerico. Do you think it was Craig who made that call?" she murmured, kissing him again.

"That's what I strongly suspect. But that's all behind us now. I spent the entire time I was flying down here jotting down some of the things we can do to help us get through the bad times, and there will be some bad times, all marriages have them." He sat up in the bed and switched the lamp on beside the bed.

Keely blinked at the shaft of painful light. "Tyler, do we have to talk about this right now?" She leaned back over and draped her arm around his neck, nibbling at his earlobe playfully. "I don't want to talk . . . not now. . . ."

Tyler ignored her seductive kisses as he rummaged around in his discarded pants pocket and withdrew a large sheet of paper. "We talk right now, then we'll"—he winked at her broadly—"do what you want to later."

Tilting her head to one side, she slanted a look at him and the large piece of paper he was holding. "Did you say you wrote a rough draft of a book, or is that really some of the suggestions you jotted down?"

"These are some A-1 ideas from some people who happen to deal with our kinds of problems every day, Keely.

Now, listen to this." He unfolded the paper and lay back down on the bed to read it. "First. We agree not to mention any situation that's more than a week old. Second. Whenever either one of us doesn't like something, instead of stewing about it, we're going to come right out and say it. For instance, I don't like it when you talk to me first thing in the morning. I'm always a grouch."

"Tell me about it!" Keely, trying to keep her attention focused, scurried back from a fast trip to the bathroom and reached for an apple in a bowl on the bedside table. Suddenly she was starving to death.

Tyler glanced up and grinned. "It's a good thing I brought those apples. Making love always did make you hungry, didn't it?"

"A week of not eating has helped considerably," she said, falling back down beside him to munch contentedly on her apple. "Proceed, Dr. Freud."

"Okay. We should make a list of things we cannot stand about each other. No matter how happy a couple is, there are certain things that they do that drive each other up a wall. After we make the list, we destroy it. But at least it will help get it out of our systems."

Keely glanced at him skeptically and took another bite of her apple.

"Next, we need to talk about other things than business when we go to bed, or all the problems we had that day. It's good to be able to do that, but we need to tell each other more how we feel about each other than what we did that day. Then we have got to stop listening to all the people who want to give us their advice. You know yourself that if that friend of yours . . . what's her name?"

"Phyllis?"

"Yeah, Phyllis. If she hadn't kept telling you not to put up with my jealousy . . ."

Keely reached up and kissed him again.

"Now, remember, we're just discussing this in a logical manner. I've already decided to not listen to anyone, when it comes to our problems." He kissed her back urgently, his hand reaching out to cup her breast tenderly. "Don't distract me; I want to finish reading this to you."

"Must you?"

"I must."

"Tyler, how many suggestions do you have?"

"Quite a few."

Keely groaned and bit into the apple again.

"Now, we should start observing more how our friends seem to keep happy marriages. Take Chris and Pam, for instance. Now, they argue, but they have something else going for them. We need to take a lesson from them about how to have differences, yet still have a happy marriage. Also, there is no reason *one* of us has to be right *all* the time. We need to learn to give in once in a while, even if *you* are wrong."

Keely cocked an eyebrow at him questioningly. "If *I'm* wrong?"

"Well, you know what I mean," he said, dismissing her question irritably. "Okay. Don't expect me to be a mind reader. If you're mad at me, try at least to give me some sort of clue about what I've done wrong!"

"You seem to be referring to me more often than you. Is that what this article said?"

Tyler leaned over and kissed the tip of her nose, his eyes still glued to his scratchy handwriting on the paper. "No, sweetheart, it's talking about both of us. I'm just using you as an example."

"Thanks!"

"You're welcome. We're going to have to maintain some independence from each other. I know I'm too possessive of you, and you're going to have to stop getting mad when I want to pursue some of my hobbies. We need time for other things in our lives, then what we have together will be just that much more enjoyable. All right. We're going to start getting away more together. We're going to go to a motel every once in a while and maybe get downright wild!"

"Terrific!" Keely sat up and took more notice of what he was saying now.

"Now, seriously, we're going to hang in there instead of getting mad and flying off the handle; we're going to sit down and discuss our problems. Divorce may be the answer for some people, but it isn't our answer, honey. I love the hell out of you, and we're going to make this relationship work or I'm going to know the reason why. And the last point, but not the least: Divorce is easy; staying together is the challenge. When I promised to love you till death do us part, I meant it, Keely. You're the only thing I've ever had in my life that was good and stable. I don't want ever to lose you. In our marriage the good far outweighs the bad. We can learn to live together and hold our tempers, or let them out and still love each other. Don't throw that apple core on the table. It'll eat the varnish off the wood. How many times have I told you that?" he said sharply, retrieving the apple core she had lain down on the bedside table and pitching it in the waste can.

"Oh, I'm sorry," she said, ashamed, "that's a bad habit I have."

"Don't worry about it, honey. I've got a lot of bad habits myself," he said as his arm came back around her and drew her close. "What I'm trying to say is, we're going to make it together, Keely Jerico. Life's too short not to spend it with someone you love. And make no mistake about it, I have enough love for both of us."

"I know you do. And I love you too." She snuggled against him contentedly.

"There's one more thing I think we should do as soon as possible."

"What's that?" She was beginning to grow drowsy and cozy in his arms.

"Your dad has been wanting a grandbaby for a long

182

time now. Don't you think we ought to start doing something about that?"

"A baby? Well, sure. You want to start now?"

Tyler chuckled and pulled her closer. "Can I take a raincheck on that. At least for an hour?"

They exchanged another long kiss, knowing that there would always be problems in their marriage, but more than willing to face them together.

"There's one more thing. Where're those damn divorce papers," Tyler said irritably.

"In my purse, why?"

"Go get them."

"Tyler!"

"Now look, you're not going to go through with this divorce . . ."

"No, of course not. But why do you want the papers right now?"

"Just please go get them . . . darling."

Within minutes she was back and handed him the papers. He drew her down beside him once more, his serious steady gaze meeting hers, his voice growing husky and poignant. "I, Tyler, take thee, Keely, for my wedded wife, to live together in the holy state of matrimony. I will love you, comfort you, honor and keep you, in sickness and in health," his voice grew to a whisper now, "forsaking all others, keep you only unto myself so long as we both shall live."

Tears blurred her vision as she reached up and traced the outline of his beloved face. "I, Keely, take thee, Tyler, as my wedded husband, to live together in the holy state of matrimony. I will love you, comfort you, honor and keep you, in sickness and in health, forsaking all others, keep you only unto myself so long as we both shall live."

"It's a new beginning for us, Keely. I won't blow it this time."

"We both will work at this marriage, Tyler. I love you."

"I love you too. May I kiss the bride?"

183

"I thought you'd never ask," she smiled through a veil of misty tears.

Their gaze locked lovingly as Tyler tore the divorce papers into tiny pieces and tossed them into the air, letting the confetti fall on their heads as their mouths met in a sweet reaffirmation of their sacred vows.

Keely was sure that she could smell the flowers, hear the pipe organ, and feel the undeniable presence of God as she kissed her husband with the fervor of a woman who had finally captured her man.

"You know, we really should have done something about this bedroom too. It needs to be painted. I never have liked this shade of blue." Tyler yawned as he snuggled back down with her still in his arms.

"Blue? This isn't blue. It's green," Keely murmured, kissing his dimple lovingly.

"Green? Keely, if this room is green, grass is blue."

"Green mist. That's the name of the paint. I ought to know, I was the one who had to go down and buy it."

"Blue Bayou. Just like the song. I remember it as clear as the day you bought it. I was the one who had to put it on the walls."

"Are you crazy, Tyler!" Keely sat up and glared at him. "Green Mist! Don't you remember the salesman telling us that this particular color of green would go nicely in a bedroom?"

"There you go again! I distinctly remember him saying that this was one of the most restful shades of blue that you could put in a bedroom." Tyler crossed his arms stubbornly.

"I can't believe you," she said, lying back down and jerking the cover back over them angrily. "If you happen to recall, we spent one whole afternoon arguing over this same stupid subject, and we never did agree on whether it was blue or green. Who cares!"

"I don't really care," he said in a more apologetic tone.

"It's just that I'm sure it was called Blue Bayou. Just like the song."

"Let's just drop the subject, okay?" She closed her eyes in agitation. Blue Bayou! It was Green Mist, or her name wasn't Keely Jerico!

There was complete silence in the room for the next five minutes as each of the occupants of the bed lay staring up at the ceiling thoughtfully. Finally Keely said in a meek, relenting voice, "Maybe it was called Blue Mist."

Tyler reached out and patted her hand. "You know, I was just lying here thinking the same thing. Blue Mist, yes, I'm sure of it." He yawned again. "Let's decide on a nice, safe purple next time."

"I think purple would be fine," she said in return, patting his hand reassuringly.

He rolled over, and she snuggled the curves of her body into the contours of his. His voice came to her in a deep husky whisper as he patted her bare bottom affectionately. "In the words of a famous poet, Mrs. Jerico, 'Grow old along with me, the best is yet to be.' "

"I'll be here," she replied evenly. And she would.

Match point!

Candlelight
Ecstasy Romances™

$1.95 each

At your local bookstore or use this handy coupon for ordering:

| **Dell** | DELL BOOKS
P.O. BOX 1000, PINE BROOK, N.J. 07058-1000 | B110B |

Please send me the books I have checked above. I am enclosing $ _____ [please add 75c per copy to cover postage and handling]. Send check or money order—no cash or C.O.D.'s. Please allow up to 8 weeks for shipment.

Name _____

Address _____

City _____ State/Zip _____

Candlelight
Ecstasy Romances™

$1.95 each

Candlelight

Ecstasy Romances™

$1.95 each

$2.50 each

The primitive new world of these lovers was like their passion— savage and untamed.

This first book in the *New Zealander* series sweeps through exotic New Zealand with a tale of adventure and passion. It is the story of William Pollard, a deserter from a British warship, and Tairata, a beautiful Maori princess. Together they embark on a perilous journey through a primitive land. 11125-0-99 $3.95

The CASTAWAY

Aaron Fletcher